BAD KARMA

BAD KARMA

A DAVID SPAULDING MYSTERY

MARY WICKIZER BURGESS

WILDSIDE PRESS

Acknowledgment

To Russell Reynnells for providing expert martial arts advice

Dedication

To Michael, As Always

ONE

Charlie was a monster.

Charlie was so certain he was a monster because his very own grandmother had told him he was. And she would know, wouldn't she? After all, he had lived with her his whole life long. So she absolutely must know all the dirty truth about him.

Charlie never knew his mother. She had died, Granny said, the very same day he had been dragged, screaming and yelling, into this evil world. And Granny had told him, over and over, that the very fact of his birth was one of the main reasons—among many others—that he was a monster. His mother had been pure as the driven snow, Granny insisted, until *he* came along. But all because of him she had become evil. And that was why God, in his greater wisdom, had taken Charlie's mother away from them.

Charlie often wondered about his mother and what she had been like. There were no pictures of her in the little cabin in the woods he shared with Granny. She had burned them all, every last single one of them, on the day he was born. But still Charlie imagined her coming back to them one day as a beautiful angel, pure again and evil no more. If only she had lived they would have been together, happily, forever after, he thought—just like in a fairy tale. And they, the two of them, would have run far, far, away from Granny and all her incessant talk of evil and wrongdoing.

Yes, Charlie decided. Everything in his life would have been wonderful and beautiful again, if only his sainted angel mother had flown back to him from Heaven and saved him from becoming such an evil monster.

He was also curious about who his father had been and whatever had happened to him. For instance—what was his name? And had he, too, died when Charlie was born? But Charlie had only dared to ask these questions about his father one time.

Then Granny flew into an angry raging fit. It was truly the very worse one he had ever seen her have—and she had had some lulus in his lifetime. This time she cuffed his head, dragged him by the ears into the little washroom they shared, and then scrubbed his mouth out with her harsh homemade lye soap until his whole throat burned.

And then she warned him on penalty of *death* never *ever* to speak of such filth again.

So he hadn't dared to ask any more questions about his background. And especially did he never ask again anything about his unknown father. But still, way down deep inside his soul, he could not stop wondering about it all. Had his father been an evil monster, too? Could *he* have been the cause of his mother's downfall?

More importantly, was Charlie *like* his father?

Granny's neighbors there on the edge of the woods didn't care much for Charlie, either. They especially did not want him hanging about their place after they caught him doing that *thing* to their big white tomcat, the one that used to lie out on Granny's tin shed roof in the sun. In fact they warned his grandmother, in no uncertain terms, that *no way* was he ever to come on to their property again—or they'd report the both of them to CPS—whatever the heck that was.

Granny had whipped him good and hard for putting the two of them in the terrible CPS jeopardy—so he never went anywhere near the Jones's place again after that.

Instead, he steered way clear of all the neighbors and spent most of his time hanging around in the wooded areas bordering on the National Forest—way out behind Granny's cabin.

There he observed nature in the wild—all the plants and animals—and especially the tiny little critters who lived under the leaves and hidden away in the crooks of rotting logs.

Those beings held a special charm for him. They were so small and vulnerable—and he was so much larger and stronger—that he could trap and cage them and control their every movement if he so desired. He began spending as much of his time as he could back there in the scrub oaks, creating magic little kingdoms and complicated games and tests to compare his captives' relative strengths and weaknesses.

And he, Charlie, was always the strongest—and Master of them all. His imaginary universe truly had become the only area of his life where he felt completely in control of his own existence.

As time passed, the day finally came for him to begin school. He had been curious about it, and had even looked forward to it in a way, as if he were embarking on an exciting new adventure.

But after that very first day, with all the other kids bullying and taunting him, and with the teacher allowing it all to go on unchecked, he knew he wouldn't—*couldn't* continue going there for the long haul.

And, just as he predicted, once the new session started up again after the holidays, Granny yanked him right out of that school. Then she went straight down to the school board, got all the paperwork, and wrote in big black letters "HOME-SCHOOLED" across the front of it.

And that was the end of that. The school authorities never did look into their situation and nobody ever came by to check to see what he was learning—or even if Granny was actually teaching him anything at all.

And that was just fine as far as they both were concerned.

He went to bed and got up when he felt like it, wore whatever clothing came to hand, dirty or clean, neat or ragged, and when he got hungry he ate whatever food he found in the kitchen.

Granny, for her part, no longer had to worry about putting together proper school clothes or packing school lunches for him, or any of that nonsense. So home schooling was a solution of sorts for her, too.

Not that any of it really mattered in the long run. Charlie might be a monster, but he wasn't *stupid*. He couldn't remember not knowing how to read, and he was adept at figuring with numbers as well.

School, with all its rules and restrictions, would have been just a hindrance to his otherwise free spirit.

And, contrary to what one might expect, every week or so, he made a point of showing up at the local library. It wasn't a *real* library, though, only the lending kind. But it contained books, all the same. And if there was anything that fascinated Charlie, other than his tiny defenseless critters, it was books.

Mrs. Crenshaw was the librarian. She had been a public school teacher for most of her life. When she retired from the school system she looked around for something she could still do in the community. And then she had a brilliant idea. She opened up her big living room in her house across the street from the school, had shelving installed on all the walls, and loaded those shelves up with books—all kinds of books—for every reading level.

All the local school children were permitted and even encouraged by their teachers to visit Mrs. Crenshaw's lending library every week and borrow her books. But she wouldn't allow them to borrow any new books until they had brought back the ones from the week before.

That rule never bothered Charlie any. He was a fast reader, and once he had read a book he never wanted to bother with it again.

So he and Mrs. Crenshaw got along just fine. She lent, he borrowed and returned, and she lent some more.

In fact, they had a great relationship and she never once acted like she thought he was a monster at all. She became the one bright light in his otherwise dismal existence.

And, not surprisingly, of all the people in their small mountain community, Mrs. Crenshaw was the one who was most shocked at what eventually happened to Charlie and his grandmother.

"I just didn't see it coming," she said, her voice quivering, when she was interviewed by the authorities about the disaster.

"I only wish I had known how bad things were in that house. Maybe I could have done something to prevent it."

But that was after the fact. And the truth was, there was probably nothing anyone in that town could have done to prevent the tragedy before it happened.

* * * *

"In the beginning was the Fire, and the Fire was with God, and the Fire was God."

Charlie was just heading into his teenage years when he discovered the Fire, when it first spoke to him—and when he *became* the Fire.

It was God, for sure, who worked the miracle. For it was He who took Charlie by the hand and it was He who led him and showed him where to look.

And it was right there in fact, in a hidden cubicle at the back of Granny's desk, that Charlie found the thick round glass set within a metal circle.

He knew immediately that the circle was a sign. It was a true sign—sent from the Almighty Lord on High.

Charlie had no business, of course, sneaking through his grandmother's things without her permission.

But every day around noon, when she stretched out like a little gray kitty-cat to take her nap on the day bed in the corner of the sitting room—Charlie knew then that his spirit was set free to roam through the house unchecked, And he did so, carefully and quietly, opening up and perusing the contents of all of his Granny's private hidey-holes, including the special ones at the back of her desk, hoping to find—what?

Did she keep any previously undisclosed information about him locked away there? Was there anything of interest at all about his unknown and unknowable parents stuffed away in those cubby-holes?

He wasn't always sure of the significance of all the bits and pieces he discovered hidden away in those secret places, but he was compelled by the endless possibility that he might find something—*anything*—that would give him answers to all the endless questions which kept smoldering away down deep inside him.

Then, on that fateful day, he found the magnifying glass—and it felt like a very great discovery, indeed. Carefully he removed it from its hiding place, wrapped in a soft chamois cloth, and carried it outside to examine it more closely in the bright sunlight.

What could this thing be? he asked himself, turning it over and over in his unwashed hands *What is this strange piece of glass? Is it a magic amulet of some sort*?

Then he saw how it caught the light and changed the rays of the sun into dancing prisms of shine and color.

Oh, how wondrous, he thought, *are the works of the Lord*!

But he had been taught that God never talks to menfolk in any straight-line way. *God only helps those who help themselves.* That's what Granny always said.

And she would know of course.

So he carried that precious magnifying glass far off into the woods where he couldn't be spied upon. And he held it up, this way and that, as he tried to figure it all out—what God—what *He* might have intended by gifting Charlie with this strange and magical implement.

Then he had an idea.

He got down on his hands and knees and peered into the bushes through the looking glass, looking for some kind of a sign.

There, in a pile of musty leaves, he spied a carpenter ant! It was one of the lowliest of the low, but it was still one of God's creations. And he watched in amazement as it increased in size through the glass—and then, as the lens caught the light of the sun, the ant bowed down its wee head before its Master—and then it smoked and burnt itself to a crisp.

It actually burnt itself all up! And it happened right before his very eyes! And because it had performed that miracle before him, Charlie became convinced that he was now the agent of God!

Yes he, *Charlie*, had become the Chosen One to sit at the right hand of God! He had been granted the power to cast death and destruction down upon an Evil World!

For without death there is no life, thus sayeth the Lord.

And so Charlie had sacrificed the ant unto the eternal glory of God, and God had smiled back. Yes, He had smiled back at *him*, Charlie!

Experimenting further, he turned the face of the glass down upon the dry grass and leaves and saw smoke rise up into the Heavens. And from that steamy smoke a mighty offering did he pledge.

Make me Thy bonded servant, Oh Lord, make me Thy Instrument, and I will do Thy will, forever and ever, Amen.

And just as he was making this promise, Charlie witnessed the finger of the Lord reach straight down from the sky and tap the ground in front of him.

A small orange figure popped up and poked its tiny head out of the brush. And then it grew and grew and *grew*.

And then it became the *Fire*!

Charlie stepped back and his mouth was opened wide in awe.

God—and his instrument Charlie—had made this powerful thing together, the two of them, out of thin air and transparent light and dense black smoke.

He stood and watched as the Fire burned up high around him. He stood right there in the very middle of that circle and watched it sweep all before it, hearing, yet not quite hearing, Granny screaming out from where she stood behind their tiny house down the hill.

"Charlie! Help me!"

But he chose to ignore her plaintive pleas for assistance, just as she had always ignored his cries for help for all his life up to that very moment—as the flames grew higher and higher around them, eating away at the cabin they called home—and snuffing out everything he despised.

Eventually her voice faded away with the curling black smoke and the floating gray ashes.

And then he knew! *He knew*! Yes, he turned himself around and around, dancing wildly within the circle and he knew!

"In the beginning was the Fire, and the Fire was with God, and the Fire was God."

TWO

He couldn't be sure at first that the thing he had spotted bobbing out there on the ocean was what he thought it was. But, as he guided his boat closer, he could see it was indeed a woman. She was way out here in the Caribbean, swimming right along, almost as if she was doing laps in a heated pool on vacation at some ritzy resort.

"Hey there lady!" he called out as he drew up next to her. "Are you all right? Do you need a lift?"

"Are you offering?" she yelled back at him. Her voice was surprisingly strong, in spite of her strenuous efforts.

He came to and put the motor in idle before throwing out a rope to her. She snagged it and wrapped it snugly around her waist before pulling herself hand over hand, toward the boat.

It looked to him as though she might have done this sort of thing before.

He hung out the ladder over the side, helped her climb aboard, and handed her one of his old deck towels so she could dry off.

"Thanks for stopping," she said, as if this were a commonplace occurrence for her.

"You came along at just the right time. I was getting a bit winded."

"What happened to you?" he said. "What in the hell are you doing on your own way out here in the middle of the ocean?"

She might very well have drowned, he thought, if he hadn't happened along just when he did. Or even worse, she could have had a very close encounter with any of the predatory sharks that had been spotted recently on the move in the area.

He was genuinely curious about the woman, of course. But in his particular line of work it didn't always pay to pry too insistently into someone else's private business.

"Our party boat sank," she said in answer to his question, gesturing vaguely back in the other direction. "So I decided to try to head for the far side of the island. It's my understanding there are a few settlers operating in and out of there. I thought maybe I could find someone with a boat and they might be willing to take me on into Florida."

She didn't offer any further explanation of exactly which of the many tiny deserted islands out here she was swimming toward. Nor did she say just whose "party" boat she had been on, where it had sunk, and—even more importantly—just what the heck she and her companions had been doing out here in this particular part of the sea.

He pondered her dilemma for a moment or so. Then he made what would be for him, a very fateful decision.

"Well, I suppose *I* could do that," he said. "I could drop you off at one of the Barrier Islands, I mean. I was just getting ready to head back in that direction. Would that be of help to you?"

He was always looking out for any kind of a payday. And this unique situation had the feel of just such a golden opportunity.

It must be serendipity, he thought to himself. *I'm in the exact right place at exactly the right time. I might as well see if I can cash in on it.*

The woman nodded and smiled at him.

"Oh, that would be just great if you would be willing to do that for me," she said, handing back the sodden towel.

"And I don't particularly care where you drop me off, either," she added. "I think any one of the Keys should be fine for my purposes. I'm sure I'll be able to make the further connections I'll need from there."

"You've got a deal then," he said. "Come on down to the lounge and I'll rustle us up some hot coffee. And I'm pretty sure my daughter has some clean sweats stored back in the cabin that might fit you all right,"

"Now," he added. "Let's go get you settled and a little more comfortable."

As he spoke, he found he was growing more and more curious by the minute about what this strange woman had been doing out here. But following his usual practice, he was cautious not to ask too many personal questions when she finally emerged from changing.

Once she had removed her wetsuit and donned the sweats, he could see she was an attractive woman if a bit mature. But she definitely was not his type, he decided. He liked to think of himself as a very savvy player and he preferred the company of much younger girls who were less experienced— and for that reason, more easily manipulated.

Just from her overly confidant attitude and the assurance with which she carried herself, he figured this lady had been around the track more than a few times. No doubt she would bear close watching.

He had already decided he would take her on in to the nearest of the Keys and hang around just long enough to see if she was good for any kind of reimbursement. Then he'd slip anchor and be on his way again.

He needed to head back down to Panama anyway at the end of this run. What he *didn't* need was any kind of weird complications in his life right now—especially of the female kind—to slow him down or trip him up.

As he stood there mulling over all of these ideas, the woman, without being invited, settled down next to him in one of the comfortable lounge chairs at the back of the boat. She sat there sipping at her coffee, all the while staring off into the choppy ocean as if she hadn't a care in the world.

In reality, however, her brain was going a mile a minute and she was making plans as fast as she could about how she was going to maneuver this happenstance meeting into something that could work out to her advantage.

After what she had just gone through back there on the other side of the island, she was definitely in the market for some new scheme to sink her teeth into—not to mention her unquenchable quest for anything of value that she might be able to add to her grubstake.

"How's the weather looking to you," she asked him lazily, as if they were old friends out for a pleasure cruise.

"Can you make out any storms on the horizon?"

"There's not a thing out there to worry about," he said, reaching out to refill her coffee. "By the way, do you want something to eat? I've got some sandwiches, chips, and stuff stashed away in that cooler next to you."

"No, thank you. I'm not hungry right now," she said. "I think I've had just about enough on my plate for today."

She said it in a joking manner—but neither of them laughed.

"So—what do you go by? I mean what name would you like me to call you?" he asked. "After all, if we're going to be stuck together for a day or two. 'Hey, you' doesn't seem very appropriate."

"Maureen," she lied easily, without really thinking about it. "...although most of my friends just call me 'Maurie.' And what do most people call *you*, if I might ask?"

"They call me Larry—for Lawrence" he lied right back at her, hoping she hadn't taken the opportunity while she was changing to look at any of his licenses or the boat registration on display in the lounge.

"Well, *Larry for Lawrence*," she said, smiling. "It's very nice to make your acquaintance. And now, I'm really very tired after all that physical exercise. If you can spare me a couple of blankets, I can bed down right out here on the deck. So long as the weather holds and it doesn't rain, I should be just fine."

"There's no need for you to do that," he said. "The couch in the lounge lets down into a bed. I can bunk there tonight. That way you can have the berth. It will be much more comfortable."

She smiled again. "Oh no, Larry," she said. "I wouldn't think of imposing on you like that. Thank you so much for offering, but please let me just take the couch. You've been so very kind. I don't want to put you out of your bed."

There was an uncomfortable moment before he got to his feet.

"All right," he said, finally. "Come on and I'll get the bedding out and give you a little time to get settled."

He had already shown her the tiny utility bath next to the galley. It was hardly larger than an airplane facility, but it was serviceable. And she had encountered much worse accommodations in her travels.

He handed her the extra bedding then went back up to the deck where he had a final cigarette and waited for what he thought was an appropriate time.

When he tiptoed back down through the lounge and on into his berth area, she seemed to be sound asleep already—at least her breathing was slow and heavy—as if she were asleep.

He didn't hang around to make sure.

* * * *

When he came to and crawled out of his berth the next morning, the sun was already up—and so was the woman.

He could smell bacon frying on the grill and a big pot of coffee could be heard bubbling away merrily in the galley.

He threw on his clothes from the day before and quickly joined the woman in the lounge. She had laid out a hearty breakfast on the wooden plank which did double duty as a counter.

"Please," she said. "Come help yourself to the food."

She gestured at the bounty before him. "I hope you don't mind that I took some liberties in your galley this morning."

"Nope," he said, sniffing appreciatively and grinning in anticipation. "I don't mind one little bit. I'm a lousy cook myself. It's quite a nice change to have someone around who knows what the hell they're doing in the kitchen. Oh, pardon my French!"

He grinned at her again—and this time she smiled back at him.

"No offense taken," she said.

He grabbed a plate and piled it high with scrambled eggs, bacon, and hot, buttered toast before accepting the steaming mug of black coffee she held out to him.

"I didn't know if you liked it black or with cream and sugar."

"This is fine. I usually just add a little sweetener."

She smiled at him again. "I must look a terrible sight. I'm just wondering what shade of green my hair must be by now."

"Do you color your hair?" he asked, realizing immediately that was the wrong question to ask.

"No," she said, just a little too quickly. "But after all that time I spent exposed to the ocean water yesterday—who the heck knows what toxic materials I might have come in contact with. I'll be lucky if my hair doesn't turn sky blue and purple!"

She *was* an attractive, if mature, woman, he had to admit to himself. Her hair was brownish with coppery highlights. It looked as though she might have shampooed it this morning, but he couldn't be sure. Her skin was the color of rich cream. And her eyes were the most incredible deep blue.

They sparkled like sapphires in the bright morning sun.

They continued to chat idly as they ate. At one point she got up and refilled their coffee mugs—and this time she thoughtfully added the sweetener as he had requested earlier.

"Why don't we take our coffee out on the deck?" she said. "It looks like it's going to be a beautiful day. We might as well enjoy it."

He agreed and they moved again to the lounge chairs at the rear of the boat. As they lolled there in the sun, sipping at their coffees, he began to relax a little more. She was a very good listener, he thought, asking leading questions about his life at just the right time—and he found himself enjoying their conversation immensely.

Gradually, Larry began to expand further on his life experiences, beginning with his career as a young man in the Navy followed by a brief stint with Special Forces after Vietnam. And then there was his mandatory retirement a few years ago after an on-the-job injury.

In fact, because she was such a good listener, he started bragging quite a lot about all of his adventures. And he even went so far as to relate some of the more intimate details about how he was spending his time these days—particularly in connection with the tiny island compound he had acquired just off the coast of Panama.

He realized, in fact, that he was extremely proud of all he had accomplished over his lifetime—and with Maureen's subtle urging, he found he just couldn't stop trying to impress this beautiful woman who appeared to be hanging on his every word.

All of a sudden he stopped in mid-sentence, coming to the realization that his enticing companion was, in reality, a total stranger to him. Even more alarming, he had been doing every bit of the talking. And worse even than that, he thought wildly, and contrary to his usual practice, he had revealed to her nearly everything about himself and his life, including all of the nasty little details he normally did not discuss with anyone—not even his closest friends.

And now, to complicate matters further, he was beginning to feel a bit dizzy and disoriented—almost as if he had been out on a drinking binge all afternoon.

Frantically, he struggled to sit up straight but immediately fell back, helpless and flailing, into the cushioned lounge chair.

"It will be so much better if you don't fight it," she said. "Unfortunately it doesn't take effect immediately—and I do apologize for that.

"Just relax," she continued in a soothing tone. "It should be all over in just a minute or two now."

Then he understood.

She had put something, either poison or a sleep agent, in the food or his coffee. Whatever she had used was apparently also acting like a truth serum, forcing him to spill all of his dirty little secrets out into the open.

"Is it poison?" he said. "Am I going to die? If so, there's someone I need you to contact for me."

"Yes, I know," she said. "You'd like me to contact your daughter. You've actually told me quite a bit about her. She sounds like an incredible young lady. You must be very proud of her.

"But don't worry," she added, almost as an afterthought. "I'm sure she will be properly informed of your demise—when the proper time comes.

"But right now, why don't you just lie back and try not to dwell on what is happening too much. After all, you've had a pretty good run, haven't you, *Larry*?

"It's time now to let someone else take over."

* * * *

She poured herself another cup of coffee and sat back to watch and wait. The day was calm and there still looked to be no storms in sight, and only a few fluffy white clouds floated overhead.

She had made sure to double-check the calculations on their heading this morning while he was still asleep—just to be certain he hadn't lied to her about heading for the Keys.

But sure enough, they were headed slightly southwest, more towards Nassau actually. So she had corrected to bring them in just a little closer to the Barrier Islands along the Florida Coast.

Fortunately, she knew enough about navigation to feel confident about their general direction—and they were not that far out from land in any case.

Eventually, the boat would drift in to a port of some kind or another, and once she was closer, she could make a final decision on just where to dock that would best suit her needs.

The man who had called himself Larry continued to struggle on a bit, in spite of her cautionary advice. That was fairly normal though. She wished he would just give up and accept the inevitable outcome but needless to say, that went against human nature.

This waiting was always the hardest part. She knew from past experience approximately how long it would take for the poison to finish doing its job. But, of course, some of her victims had been physically stronger than the others, so the timing was always just a guestimate at best.

At some point, inevitably, Larry's frantic spasms grew weaker and weaker until gradually they ceased altogether. Finally he lay back in the lounge chair, uttered one last long sigh—and was still at last.

The woman known as Maureen checked Larry's pulse just to be sure his heart had stopped then expertly began going through each of his pockets, emptying his wallet and searching for ID, keys, and any other crucial papers or notebooks.

When she was absolutely certain there wasn't a scrap of paper or any jewelry left on him that could identify him immediately, she rolled him off the lounge chair and with several mighty heaves, got him up over the rail and into the sea. She watched with interest as he bounced along in the wake of the boat for a bit before gradually sinking beneath the waves.

Then she turned her attention to her real work.

She checked the boat's heading one more time just to satisfy herself that the motor was still chugging away in good form. Then, quickly, she moved back into the lounge and began tearing the whole place apart.

She looked everywhere that anything of value could possibly be hidden away. The most obvious locations were quickly and expertly divested of all the usual documents: the boat registration, a deed to and property description of a tiny island off the coast of Panama, "Larry's" boat and drivers' licenses, and various other records, papers and identification.

She spent the entire rest of the afternoon poring over and organizing each of the items which might be of any possible value to her and stuffed them carefully, one by one, into an empty duffle bag she had dug out of Larry's tiny closet.

There must be something else here—she thought frantically—there had to be some real bonanza of a find.

Meticulously she began retracing her original steps, this time she tapped along all of the *faux*-wood-paneled interior walls of the cabin.

Finally she was rewarded with a distinct and familiar hollow echo. Using tools from a box stored in the engine room, she carefully began prying away the flimsy fiberboard paneling until she uncovered a hidden pocket hidden between the studs—just large enough to hold a small safe.

She pulled it out and carried it to the table where she examined it thoroughly. It was not a particularly difficult mechanism, and she easily broke through the combination and opened it up to reveal a fat sheaf of negotiable bonds and banded currency of various denominations, some foreign—mostly Euros—and some in good old-fashioned U.S. dollars.

She sat back in relief. Here was the payday she had been seeking to add to the cash she had pilfered from the ship cabins and the tiny lethal drug packets, both hidden away in a small waterproof pouch taped to her midsection and camouflaged by her outer clothing.

When she finished counting it all up and adding in the possible values of the boat and the property in Panama, she smiled her little cat's smile.

Together with her existing stash, it would be worth a tidy sum—and now it was all hers.

Her future was now looking a whole lot brighter, but there were still just a few small problems she had to overcome. She would need to concoct a flawless back story now to explain her upcoming presence in Florida—or wherever else she decided to end up.

The story should not draw too much attention to her as an individual, but instead help her to blend seamlessly as an average person into the local population.

It would be necessary to stay put there for a while to regroup, she decided. And she also would need to think long and hard about what her next options ought to be.

After all, she could, with the resources now available to her, go almost anywhere in the world and pay her own way for quite a while.

But what she really wanted to do was get back to her home turf. To do that she decided, she had two clear choices: reenter her native country as a legitimate citizen merely returning home or, the better possibility she thought, establish a whole new identity as someone entirely different.

She could become a completely new person, with a new background, new skills, and new looks. The latter was always the easiest part to accomplish. She could change her hair color and style, artificial lenses would change the color of her eyes, and she could even have facial reconstruction if necessary.

Indeed, she was already extremely accomplished at disguise and acting in different roles. She had even, quite successfully, played the part of a man for a time. It was all in the mannerisms, the tone of voice, and in the image one projected.

Most casual observers saw only what they expected to see—not the true reality of things as they really were.

As the afternoon began to drift on toward evening, she prepared a tasty supper for herself from some of the provisions stored in Larry's little galley.

Then she ate out on deck, watching the sun gradually set toward the west. The sky turned pink then deepened into a peachy orange.

It was a beautiful sight.

And, as she watched, a rather bedraggled looking young sea bird of some kind fluttered on to the deck—right in front of her. It did not seem afraid and was obviously looking for something to scavenge for its own meal.

Taking pity on her visitor, she went to the cabin below and put together a concoction using some of the crumbs left over from the morning breakfast she had shared with her erstwhile companion.

She returned to the deck and tossed the leavings out in front of the fledgling—just a short ways from her chair—and sat down to wait and watch. Soon, the creature came forward again and, without hesitation or fear, began pecking away at her offering.

But, as it finished its repast, something strange began to happen. First the bird squawked a bit, looking up at her with something like panic in its grayish eyes. Then it began fluttering about the deck, trying to flap its wings in order to fly away, but seemingly unable to coordinate its movements.

She eyed the little drama taking place in front of her intently. It reminded her of the actions of her human victim earlier. Perhaps it was impossible for any living thing to simply relax and let the poison take its effect. Yet again, she supposed, it was the nature of all beasts to fight off an inevitable attack, once they recognized something had gone so terribly wrong.

Her feathered friend flipped and flopped about on the deck, uttering loud shrieks of pain and terror. She continued to watch it dispassionately. Her only discernible emotion was the pleasurable sense of her curiosity being satisfied, much as a researcher might monitor a lab animal's movements during a successful experiment.

Finally the bird, peeping piteously now, fluttered a few more times before stretching out in front of her perfectly still, as a supplicant would throw himself prone before his Almighty Creator.

She got up, approached the creature, and kicked at it with her bare toe. It did not respond.

She picked it up and cradled it in her arms briefly, as a mother might rock her sleeping child. Then, without further ado, she flung its lifeless body over the rail and into the ocean—where it sank without a trace.

The Western sky had now turned a vivid red. It looked as though her whole world was drenched with blood.

She smiled. She would sleep well tonight.

THREE

David Spaulding was hopelessly lost. He knew he was lost because he had been circling the mall over the past half hour and he still had seen nothing that looked the least bit familiar to him.

Finally he came to a dead stop in the middle of one of the parking aisles and sought the help of the smart lady who lived in his phone.

"Take me to The Last Chance Bar & Grill," he commanded her.

She recalculated a bit before instructing him to go to the very end of the aisle he was in and turn right. He was on it before she finished speaking and, following her directions without thinking about it too much, he rapidly accelerated out of the parking lot and sped right down the parkway for half a mile.

"Turn right into Parking Lot B," she then ordered him with an air of finality. "You have reached your destination."

And so he had.

He understood now what had happened to the facility which had once been so familiar to him. A brand new movie theatre complex, with all of its attendant satellite shops and eating places, had completely cut off the entire rear section of the shopping center from through traffic.

And here indeed, back in Parking Lot B, was his familiar old stomping ground, sitting alone, dejected and nearly abandoned, behind all of the flashy brand new buildings stacked in front of it. There were a few other establishments clinging to life here as well, including a paint store, a pet grooming service, and an auto parts supply.

And right there where it had always sat was The Last Chance Bar & Grill.

But today there were only a handful of cars parked nearby—unheard of during lunch hour on a weekday in his past memory. He wondered how in the hell any of these places were managing to keep their businesses going without the usual walk-in traffic.

He spotted a familiar car parked right in front of the bar and pulled in alongside it. He got out and stretched his tired and aching muscles.

He'd been up and on the go since early that morning—catching the commuter flight to Pittsburg out of BWI, picking up a rental car at the airport and now, for the last half hour at least, circling this damn mall while he tried to find a place he had once known like the back of his hand.

He pulled open the heavy door, entered, and paused to let his eyes adjust to the dimmed light inside.

"Would you like a table or a seat at the bar, sir?" asked a young hostess in shorts coming forward to greet him.

"No, I'm meeting someone," he said. "And I'm pretty sure they're already here."

He spotted them just as he said it and headed back to their usual booth at the back.

"Hiya, guys," he said, sliding into the bench they'd left open for him. "Have you been waiting long?"

The two seated men looked up at their former partner with smiles of welcome.

"Hey, buddy, it's about time," said the older-looking of the two, glancing at his watch. "What in the hell took you so long?"

"They've changed the mall all about," Dave said. "I must be stupid or something, but I actually had to use my phone to figure out where in blue blazes they were hiding this place."

The other two laughed.

"Oh, sure," said the second man. "I totally forgot about all that. Yeah, they really changed it up when the movie complex came in and took over most of the mall. We should have warned you, or at least given you a head's up and all. I'm really sorry about that."

"It's all right. No harm done," he said. "I finally figured it out."

He picked up the menu in front of him and began perusing it. "Is the food still good here?" he said to no one in particular.

"Now, don't go ordering a whole lot to eat," Chip Lutz said. "The girls are planning a big blowout dinner for all of us at the house tonight. They've been waiting to show off the place to you and get your take on all the changes they've been making."

"Oh, hell," Dave said, suddenly chagrined. "I'm sorry. I should have warned you ahead of time. I'm going to have to go right straight back to the airport from here. I'm booked on the red-eye, the last flight out to the coast tonight. I just wanted to touch bases with you guys and—"

Carl Frick shook his head. "The ladies are going to be very disappointed, Dave. They were really hoping to see you."

"I wasn't even scheduled to come through here," he said by way of apology. "I only made the change at the last minute—just to squeeze in this stop. I'm supposed to be on the West Coast—in San Francisco—by tomorrow. There are people out there who are expecting me."

"Well," Chip, scratched his head. "I guess I'd better give the ladies a call—let them know not to plan on you for dinner. Go ahead and order up a good meal here, then. You're going to need something to eat if you're tak-ing the red-eye all the way out to the coast. But I just wish we'd known this sooner."

"I'm really sorry," he said again. "But it just can't be helped, guys. And I may as well tell you exactly what I'll be doing out there. I've been given my first assignment and…"

But right then his cell phone buzzed. He pushed a button and examined the transmitted text message for a moment before looking up at them with a sheepish grin.

"Well, you'll never guess what's just happened," he said. "My flight's been cancelled on account of bad weather—a tornado watch in the Midwest or something. I won't be flying out of here until tomorrow morning after all. You'd better not call the ladies and cancel that dinner just yet, guys—and I think I'm going to have to beg a bed from you tonight, too."

"I'm really sorry about that," Carl said with a grin. "But I can't say I'm *really* sorry. We all were looking forward to having a little bit of time with you—just to catch up on everything that's happened, you know. I mean the way everything was left—the last time we were together—it was so up in the air."

"Yeah," Chip added. "I think we're all still reeling from how quickly everything in our lives has changed. And I can't even begin to imagine what it must have been like for you. How the hell *are* you, anyway, Dave? I mean, *really.*"

Dave had to think that last question over a bit before replying. *How was he*? He wasn't sure he could respond to his friends truthfully right now. He wasn't at all sure he knew the answer to that one himself.

He shrugged it off.

"Come on, guys," he said, laying the menu back down on the table. "Let's get out of here. I'm going to have to get an early start in the morning and I'd much rather spend the time I've got left talking with you and the ladies then sitting here in this godforsaken place."

He signaled the waitress, apologized for their sudden departure, and handed her a twenty dollar bill before leaving the Last Chance. They re-trieved their respective cars and headed out of Parking Lot B toward the mansion that had once belonged to Conrad Emerson, David Spaulding's old boss and mentor.

As he drove, he thought about what changes the two couples might have made to the place although, truthfully, he really didn't care all that much. No one had been more surprised than Dave when, following the con-sequences which resulted from the disastrous sinking of the cruise ship *Nerissa* he had been informed he was Connie's sole heir.

Not knowing what else to do about the situation, as he completed his plans to leave Pittsburgh to join the FBI, he had signed the necessary paperwork leaving the place in charge of Chip and Carl and their wives.

Not only had Connie, his mentor and father figure, died in the disaster. David had also lost Deborah, his bride-to-be and the love of his life, when the *Nerissa* sank to the bottom of the ocean.

As a result of the trauma they had all suffered, he knew he could never return to Pittsburgh, to work or to live. Someone might as well make use of the property he reasoned—and who better than his oldest and most trusted friends?

Still, as they drew near Connie's old stomping grounds, he felt an unaccustomed sense of nostalgia.

And as he stepped out of the car and looked once more on the imposing façade, it almost felt like coming back home.

It almost felt the same—but not quite.

Two women in their mid-thirties stepped out on the front porch to welcome him.

"Hi, Rachel," he said, giving her a hug. "Doreen. How's it going?"

She grinned at him.

"So the guys roped you in after all," she replied. "And it's a good thing, too. We went all out on dinner. And we really don't want all that effort wasted on these mugs."

He laughed and followed them in to the foyer.

He looked about and nodded approvingly. They had definitely made some changes for the better in what once had been a somewhat old-fashioned décor.

He glanced into the living room just beyond.

"Wow! You *have* gone all out, haven't you?"

Rachel shifted nervously at his words.

"Is it all right?" she asked anxiously. "Did we go over the top? Because, you know, we can always…"

"Nonsense!" he laughed again. "This is great! I could have never figured all this out on my own."

The walls of the living area had been painted in fresh bright colors, predominately pale blues and greens with accents of white on the woodwork. The entire effect was both soothing and eye-catching at the same time.

"We didn't make too many changes in *your* quarters, though," Rachel went on hurriedly. "We weren't sure just what colors you might like, so we tried to stay more with neutrals in there. Do you want to take a look at it? Get freshened up before dinner?"

"No, I'm fine," he said. "And I have a very early flight tomorrow, so I'll need to be up and out of here. We should probably go ahead and eat whenever you're ready. I have some things I want to discuss with you all. We might as well have that conversation around the table."

The others glanced at each other nervously, wondering what in the world this discussion would entail—and what it might mean for their collective futures.

Following the unexpected death of his old mentor, Conrad Emerson, David Spaulding understandably had been shocked to find that Connie had left his entire estate, including this house, to him. And David's friends were equally shocked when he suggested they take over the property for their own use.

"What are you talking about?" Chip had said. "The place is yours, Dave, and rightfully so. Why in the world don't you just come on back here and enjoy some much needed down time. Of course, we'll help you get settled—in whatever way we can. But, man, this place is *yours*, and that's what Connie wanted. Don't throw it all away without thinking it over."

But David had thought it over. He had no desire to continue living in the setting where so much had gone wrong. The decision to take the ill-fated cruise had been one of the worst ideas of his life. He was in no mood now to compound the mistake.

"My mind's already made up," he had said. "I'm not going to be coming back here to live. At least I'm not going to do it in the near future. I'm taking a new direction with my life. The offer from the FBI is just too good to turn down. If I'm successful in that program, I suspect I'm going to be sent out on assignment, more often than not. In the meantime, there's no point in this beautiful place sitting here empty and going to waste.

"What do you want me to do?" he added, almost as an afterthought. "Shall I sell the place? What would that achieve? You're my best—no— you're my *only* friends left here. I can see you in Connie's old place—enjoying what he worked so hard to achieve. It would give me more pleasure than I can express to you, to know I had, for maybe the very first time in my life, made the *right* decision."

And that was where they had left it. Of course the two couples had been overwhelmed with his generosity. But, on a deeper note, he felt they truly understood why this was a good outcome—to what had started out as a very unhappy situation.

Now, here he was, back again to the scene of the crime, he thought wryly. But there was some satisfaction, at least, in witnessing how well this had all worked out—for all of them.

"When do we eat?" he said suddenly. "I'm starving. And I suspect there is something very good waiting for us at the table tonight."

* * * *

He allowed himself one glass of wine only from Conrad's special store in the cellar.

"Sure you don't want a top-off?" Carl said. "We can't let this one go to waste, you know."

"It's not going to go to waste, and you know it," Dave replied. "I have to get out of here early in the morning, though, and I don't want to start that long trip with a sore head."

He waited until they all were holding their glasses up. "To our absent friends," he said. "And may they both be at rest in eternal peace."

The others murmured assent then Doreen began passing heaping platters of food around.

"We just put it together family style," she said. "I hope you enjoy what we chose…"

"It all looks great," Dave said. "I'm starving, and this will be the best meal I've had in a very long time."

There was a moment of silence while plates were passed back and forth and filled, and china and silver clinked.

Finally, when they all were seated and eating, Dave began to speak.

"I wanted to tell you all a little bit at least about my new assignment. It's exciting, really. I'm off to San Francisco tomorrow. I'll have a day or so before checking in with my contact in California. But after that, I'll be going completely undercover. I thought you all ought to know that—just in case…"

"What are you saying?" Rachel interrupted. "Are you going to be in any kind of danger? I don't like the sound of this."

He paused, swirled the last bit of wine in his glass and took a final sip.

"In this line of work, as we all know, there's always a certain element of uncertainty. But no, I don't think I'm going to be putting myself in the kind of danger you're thinking of. It's just that since the State of California covers a lot of territory, I'm not going to be able to predict just where I'll be at any particular time—and where this assignment might end up taking me. So I'm going to need to be flexible and go wherever the investigation leads me."

"In that case, is there anything we can do to help you—on this end of it, I mean? You know, like looking up records and information—that sort of thing?" Chip regarded him anxiously. "After all, I used to be pretty good at finding out stuff like that."

"Maybe," Dave said. "And I'll certainly let you know if that's the case. But I think mostly I'll just be observing—looking for patterns—anything that seems odd or out of line. Since I'll going in undercover, I'll be posing as a local tourist—taking in the sights and asking the usual dumb touristy questions of the locals."

"You say you're flying out to San Francisco? Will you have a chance to see Richard? Or will that be off limits, given your undercover status?"

Doreen was speaking now of Richard Black Wolf, a well-known author and anthropologist whom they had gotten to know on the cruise ship. He and David Spaulding had formed an instant rapport, and Richard had been instrumental in the final overthrow of the terrorists during their attempt to scuttle the *Nerissa*.

"Yes, as a matter of fact I will see Richard. He'll be picking me up at the airport and I'm going to stay at his apartment for the first couple of days. And believe me I fully intend to take advantage of our time together to pick his brains about this assignment. As we all well know, he's pretty damn good at figuring out the criminal mind. I'm hoping he might be able to give me some further insight into just what's going on with this particular perp—or perps. We're not sure if the culprit is working with an accomplice yet."

"Well, at least you'll have somebody there on your side to help. I hope you'll be able to stay in touch with him, even if you are going undercover." Carl shook his head. "I'd feel a whole lot better if you had some back up. This all sounds like it might be dangerous. I hope I'm wrong about that."

Dave paused. Here was the opening he was looking for, but suddenly he felt reluctant about even bringing it up.

"Which," he said. "…gets us to what I wanted to talk to you about this evening."

A penny could have been heard if it had been dropped in that moment on the highly-polished hardwood floor beneath their feet

"I've been given leeway to bring in one or two trusted and experienced associates to provide back up for me on this assignment…"

There was an almost audible intake of breaths around the table.

"Of course, you two were the first people I thought of," Dave said to his old comrades on the police force. "It would require that you travel to California independently—and undercover obviously. Once there, you would go to various different locations posing as vacationers, where you would gather and provide whatever additional observations and information you can about the situation in question. You'd be two more pairs of eyes on the ground for me."

"How long would we be out there, do you think?" Carl asked.

"That part is uncertain. Certainly it would be for as long as my superiors deem necessary to get the job done. And, of course, you would be paid by the government—and fairly well I might add."

The two women looked at each other. Rachel sighed. "I guess we two can handle things here on the home front for the duration. What do you think, Doreen? Can we hold down the fort?"

Doreen smiled. "You bet we can! And don't you guys worry one little bit about us. We'll look after each other and the place. We'll be just fine."

Dave was a little surprised at the women's willingness to let their men take on such a proposal—although, he realized, he shouldn't have been. These ladies were quite capable of taking care of themselves and everything else here at home.

Chip and Carl looked at each other. "How soon would we have to let you know our decision?" Chip asked.

"As soon you can, of course. But I understand this would be a huge undertaking—for all of you. I can fill you in on all the details before I leave here. But I won't expect you to make a final decision right away.

"Take a few days to talk it over. You can let me know while I'm still at Richard's. In fact, I'm going to ask him if he will sign on to act as a sort of liaison for me—for all of us—if you agree to do this. We know we can trust him, and I'm positive he will do everything in his power to keep us safe and in contact with each other."

"All right," Carl said. "I'm willing to look at your proposal. I think I've been getting a bit stagnant, just lying around here and letting these good ladies wait on me all the time."

He grinned at Doreen and Rachel to let them know he was kidding.

"Me, too," Chip added. "We sort of make a team, the two of us. Sounds like this might be just the ticket for getting us out of the doldrums, so to speak."

"'All right," Dave said. "Now, everything I say here will have to be committed to memory. Once out there in California, I won't be able to have much contact with either of you, at least not on a regular basis. We can probably set up meets if necessary. But I think our best bet will be to run everything through Richard. From what I understand, he's been itching for some new project to sink his teeth into as well."

"Do you need us to leave the room while you talk about this?" Rachel asked.

"No, you absolutely do not need to leave." Dave shook his head. "You two deserve to be every bit an integral part of this operation. And if I can't trust the four of you—"

He didn't need to say any more. Doreen reached over and patted his hand.

"You can trust us with your life, Dave. And that's a guarantee."

* * * *

Bright and early the next morning, Dave, carry-on in hand, made his way into the kitchen where he was greeted with coffee, a banana, and a bowl of steaming oatmeal.

When he protested, Rachel shook her head.

"You may not get a chance to eat anything before you get on the plane," she said. "And this is going to be a long day for you. Humor me and eat a few bites anyway. It'll stick to your ribs."

He laughed. "I haven't heard that term in a very long time. All right, I'll try to force it down."

So saying, he grabbed the bowl and wolfed down the cereal in a few minutes. It tasted surprisingly good.

"Thanks," he said, raising his cup of coffee in salute. "You're right, of course. That hit the spot. And at least I have something solid and nourishing on my stomach.

"And now, I really do have to hit the road. I have no idea what kind of traffic I'll be facing. And I still have to turn the car in."

"We could drive you," Chip offered. "We could turn the car in for you."

"No, I think it's better if I do it myself. It's a government rental. Someone might make a stink about it and that would throw everything off.

"Now," he added. "You've got everything straight?"

The two men nodded assent.

"Good. I'll be in touch with you from Richard's place as soon as possible. Once I'm there and checked in, I'll go ahead and firm up your assignments again with my bosses and get your pay and travel vouchers scheduled."

He paused and looked at them seriously. "Remember. If either of you has any hesitations at all, you're free to back out at any time. Don't forget that. I won't hold you to anything. And I'll understand if you decide this little adventure isn't for you."

"Don't worry about us, boss," said Carl. "We talked about it again this morning—all of us..." he glanced at the women. "We're on board for the long haul. And we'll have no regrets, I promise you that."

A film came over Dave's eyes. These were truly good people—and good friends.

"Thanks, guys," he said, his voice cracking just a bit. "This means the world to me. I want you all to know just how much I appreciate what you're all doing."

Doreen and Rachel stepped forward and delivered big hugs and kisses.

"Never mind all that," Doreen said. "You just take care of yourself, you big lug. Don't go taking any foolish chances now."

Chip and Carl each shook his hand. "And don't forget," Chip said. "We're going to be providing you the best backup you've ever had in your life."

He saluted them solemnly, then turned and strode out into the dawn.

He was on his way into a brand new chapter of his life. Time would tell if he had made the right decision this time.

* * * *

David Spaulding stood quietly near the front of the A list line waiting to board his non-stop flight to San Francisco. It was early enough in the morning that many of the shops and restaurants in the terminal were still not open, so he was glad he had taken his friends up on their breakfast offer.

He would be working undercover during his assignment in California, but because he was a Federal agent the boarding attendant and plane crew had been made aware of his status. His instructions were to stay low-key and out of the way for the duration of the flight if at all possible. He would not interfere in any minor disturbance or infraction in the cabin, but leave it to the very capable on-board staff to handle.

Only if there was some sort of threat of a more serious or terrorist nature would Dave offer to step in to help out. He sincerely hoped that would not be the case and looked forward, instead, to a quiet uneventful flight where he might be able to grab a couple more hours of sleep.

There were several people waiting in wheelchairs near him as the boarding agent began her announcements.

"If there are any of you traveling in wheelchairs who believe you are capable of walking the short distance down the ramp for boarding it would be much appreciated," she said. "We're a little short-handed at this time and it would speed up our boarding operation tremendously."

There was a little buzz amongst the invalids and their caregivers. Most opted out of the request, but eventually one elderly man stepped forward, pushing his wife and holding out a pair of crutches.

"We'll give it a try," he said to the clerk who beamed at him.

"Why, thank you very much," she said with a meaningful look at the others who had not stirred from their chairs. "It's very responsible and generous of you both to make the offer.

"Go right on down as soon as you're ready," she added. "Someone at the other end will help you board." She turned away from them and back to the paperwork on her desk.

With a little hesitation and much urging from her husband, the frail woman was pulled into a standing position and the crutches thrust under her arms. Teetering on her feet, and guided by her husband's firm hand on her elbow, she began, very slowly, to negotiate the carpeted but bumpy ramp down to the plane cabin door.

Dave sighed. What was wrong with these idiots? Did they actually believe people were using wheelchairs on purpose just to be first on the plane? He felt like offering his assistance to the couple, but the trickiness of his situation forced him to hold back.

Still, he found himself steeling for disaster as the couple painfully and slowly clunked their way down the ramp. Then, just as he had feared, as they rounded the final bend, the old lady did a header, *Boom!* right down on the hard surface.

It took the clerk a moment to realize what had happened before she dropped her work and went running down to help. Staff from the plane hurried out to assist the woman as well, but it was obvious she had been badly injured.

Those like him who had witnessed the bungled boarding were quiet for the most part, but Dave sensed the overall mood of resentment. The accident had been so unnecessary and for what? If anything, the flight would now be delayed much beyond the few minutes it would have taken to escort all the wheelchairs down safely.

Finally, after EMT staff had come and gone with the lady removed on a gurney, and her husband trailing sadly behind, boarding resumed. All in all, it had probably taken another half an hour or more to sort things out.

As he boarded and took his seat near the front, he overheard the crew discussing the situation.

"Damned shame," the pilot said. "But there was no way I could allow her to stay on board. She could have had a concussion or internal bleeding. It would be irresponsible to overlook that. I really had no choice but to ask her to leave the plane."

The steward nodded. "What I can't understand," he said. "…is why they were allowed to try and walk down the ramp alone like that. She could have been killed. It's a real liability issue for the airline. Whoever is responsible should be fired on the spot."

Dave considered speaking up to add his protest to theirs but again thought better of it, considering his undercover status. It would not be a good idea to get drawn in as a witness to some sort of protracted civil suit.

No, he thought. Better to let sleeping dogs lie.

* * * *

Eight hours later at four o'clock his time (although only 1 p.m. California time) his plane taxied to a stop and after the usual bumping and grinding of locks and doors, the passengers were welcomed to San Francisco and set free once more to wander off on their own.

Toting his carry-ons, Dave made his way among the other weary travelers to the far end of the court and down the escalator to the main terminal.

He hesitated, looking about for any sign of Richard and finally spotted his friend near one of the exits where he was waving furiously in Dave's direction.

Richard quickly joined him and grabbed one of the bags.

"Come on," he said. "I got lucky. My car's over in the main lot, and not too far off. How was the trip," he added. "You're late. Did you have any problems with the flight?"

"Nope, none whatsoever," he said. "Not once we actually got on board the plane that is."

Richard looked at him quizzically and he laughed. "Yes there was an issue, but it's not really funny. I'll tell you all about it when we get to the car."

Later, once Richard had skillfully negotiated the parking lot and all the streets leading in and out of it, Dave narrated the incident with the lady boarding the plane.

"That's sounds very incompetent to me," Richard said. "It borders on criminal negligence. I don't blame you for being steamed about it. That never should have happened."

"The trouble is," Dave said. "I felt like I couldn't voice my opinion because of my situation. This is my first undercover assignment for the Bureau. I don't want anything to go wrong—and I felt like I had to keep my mouth shut and just walk away from it."

"Understood," Richard said, glancing in his rear view mirror before crossing into another lane. "I'd feel exactly the same."

They drove along quietly for a bit then Richard spoke up. "Now, how hungry are you? I mean, would you be ready for a good meal right about now?"

"Would I ever," Dave said. "The girls filled me up with oatmeal this morning, but I haven't had anything since then except a handful of pretzels. Do you have anything in mind?"

"There's this place," Richard replied. "It's over on the shore. I only get out there once or twice a year. But believe me, the food they have there is well worth the drive."

"Lead me to it," Dave said. "It sounds like the perfect end to the day. We can talk more about what I'm doing here—and the role I'd like you to play—if you're willing that is."

"Hmm. Now that sounds like an interesting proposition—and just what would I be expected to do? Nothing illegal---or lethal—I hope!"

Dave laughed. "Not if I can help it. But, hey, given our track record, you can never be sure."

* * * *

A few hours later, Dave sat back from a luscious seafood dinner and relished the last few sips of a very good white wine. The two men had talked at length about Dave's new assignment and the fact that Chip and Carl had signed on and were now going to be joining them in a few days. Most importantly, Dave explained how he thought Richard could be of assistance to the task at hand.

"Of course," Richard said. "I'll do anything—and everything—I can within my power to help. I'm in between projects of my own right now. And who knows? This whole thing, if it turns out as we hope, might be the very thing I'm looking for as inspiration for my next book."

"You realize, of course," Dave said. "This whole affair has to be kept quiet until there is some resolution, until I am told by my bosses that we've had a successful outcome, and until I am at liberty to discuss my assignment more freely?"

"Oh, yes, of course. And I can and will abide by that prohibition. Still, you have got to admit that this whole premise is right up my alley. I mean what could be more interesting from a psychologist's point of view than the issue of arson and those responsible for it? Who commits these crimes after all? And why on earth would they do a thing?"

"That's exactly what I've been thinking, too," Dave said. "Of all people, I figured you could not only provide a base of operations for us here, for contacting each other and for relaying messages back and forth, but I also believe you could be a very valuable resource for just the things you've mentioned—background and motive. That kind of insight might give us just the edge we need to nail this bastard."

"All right, then. Done and done," Richard said. "Now, if you've finished up the last dregs of your wine (he had abstained beyond a sip because he was driving), I suggest we get back to my apartment *tout suite* and start putting together some strategies. I already have some ideas..."

Richard was an idea man at heart, and he enjoyed nothing more than brainstorming with his friends.

"I'm ready," Dave said. "Let's dream up some surprises for our Fire-starter. It's about time someone doused his flame."

FOUR

Their paperwork completed, Chip and Carl flew in to Oakland International Airport just a few days later and caught BART across the Bay. Richard and Dave were there to meet them at the stop in the City they had agreed upon the night before.

"Now," Richard said, as he and Dave each picked up a bag. "Have you guys ever been to San Francisco before?" Richard asked.

The two men looked at each other, shaking their heads.

"Nope, not me," said Carl "In fact, I've never been west of the Mississippi River myself. I've always wanted to visit here, though," he added, staring about in fascination at the bustling financial area "South of the Slot" where they had emerged from the Bay Area Rapid Transit train.

"Me, neither," said Chip. "But I've heard so much about this place. I'm just grateful for an opportunity to take in some new territory in my old age."

"Good," said Richard with a grin. "I think you're going to enjoy this."

So saying, he led them all up California Street where they hopped aboard the next cable car to come their way and headed off to San Francisco's fabled Chinatown for a leisurely lunch.

Richard looked over the menu and took charge of the ordering. Soon they were passing around steaming platters of food unlike anything the other three had ever experienced.

"This is sure a far cry from any of our take-out places back home," Dave commented, as he sampled the Peking duck.

"They look almost like Chinese burritos, don't they?" Chip said, holding up one of the pancakes stuffed with thin slices of crispy duck skin, green onions and *hoisin* plum sauce..

Richard snorted, trying to hold back his laughter. "I never thought of them quite like that," he said. "But I think you have a point. That's what I'm going to call them from now on—Chinese burritos!"

Conversation was kept casual while they ate, although all the recent news reports detailing the unusual number of destructive wild fires spreading up and down the state were uppermost in their minds.

After they had shared a final cup of green tea, Richard led his three friends back to the cable car stop for their final ride up Nob Hill to his apartment building.

Once inside, Carl and Chip were shown to the guest rooms to settle in, while Richard and Dave made their way to the den. The large comfortable room was now crammed with a standing white board stickered with post-it notes, a large teak conference table covered with spread out maps, yellow-lined pads and pens in multiple colors—not to mention several desk top computers and printers set up around the room.

"Wow!" said Chip, as the new visitors made their way into Richard's inner sanctum. "I'm guessing this must be the war room!"

"We tried to think of everything," Dave laughed. "We might have gone a little bit overboard though. What do you say, Carl? Does this pass muster?"

Carl was perusing the white board with great interest.

"It looks to me like you've come up with some very interesting information already," he said. "And you've only been on the job—what—one or two days now?"

"Well, Richard had gotten a bit of a head start on all this before I got here a few days ago," Dave said. "But, yeah, we've been doing quite a bit of brainstorming. Now that you two are here, I think we can come up with some even more interesting scenarios."

Richard, in the meantime, had opened a glass-encased bookcase behind his desk and was rummaging around among the textbooks stored there.

"Here," he said finally, pulling out an oversized leather volume. "This is the one I was looking for."

They all gathered around the conference table then, as Richard opened up the book to the comprehensive index at the back, rand ran his finger down one column.

"Ah," he said. "Here it is."

He thumbed to the page indicated and found his place. He began reading aloud to them bits and pieces of an abstract from an article on findings from prior year case studies involving serial arsonists. He stopped every now and then to make or listen to a comment as he read.

"In this study for example," he said. "Data were obtained from a number of incarcerated serial arsonists from several states over—hmm—looks like at least a five-year period.

"The various results confirmed that most of the offenders interviewed seemed to be white males from their teen years into their late twenties. Frequently they had serious problems in their personal lives, including poor relationships with parents or caretakers—and many of them had not completed high school. Most had prior felony arrests, serious or significant medical issues, and only a third of them were regularly employed. None were in what could be considered a professional occupation. And at least half of the perpetrators had had problems with alcohol or drug abuse at some point in their lives.

"Here's what's interesting," he added. "The most common motives they gave for the crimes they had committed were seeking revenge for past slights, thrill seeking, or a combination of both.

"So," Richard said sitting back and closing the tome with a bang. "While we mustn't assume our present suspect conforms to *every* single one of these statistics completely, I believe we at least can come up with some general assumptions."

"I think we can start looking at young, white males, mostly between the ages of 18 to 30," said Dave. "At least that's a starting point. It doesn't, of course, rule anyone else out. But it sounds to me like a valid place to begin our search." He shook his head.

"Does anyone else get the sense we are about to go on that proverbial search for a needle in a haystack?"

Carl turned back to the board again

"There's something else here that has been bothering me," he said. "All of these recent wildfires, most of them occurring over the past two to three months, are scattered about all over the state. Are we even sure it's the same individual? Or could he be working with an accomplice or a gang even? That alone might rule out some of the other theories we're looking at here."

"Well," said Richard, reviewing his notes from the abstract again. "According to this statistical study at least 'No discernible patterns were observed in the overall target selection of serial arsonists'. What that says to me is that, in most cases, the target may have been completely at random. By the way, in my experience as a psychological counselor, that theory complies with the common known patterns for serial killers as well. In fact, most of them appear to choose their victims at random—sometimes by appearance—but, and this is important, I think—their choices also seem to be based on opportunity alone.

"In other words, sometimes it *is* purely a random choice."

"Yeah," said Chip. "I'm sure I've heard that somewhere, too."

"Also," Dave said. "Another big clue might be that bit about having hostile or cold relationships with their parents or caretakers. That fact might be something else we could zero in on as well."

Richard was silent for a moment.

"Look," he said finally. "I don't want to throw cold water on this enterprise at the beginning. But unless we get real lucky here—run across some clues that not only fit this known pattern while putting the right person in all the right places at all the right times—well, I'm not sure this is even doable."

Dave stared at him stunned.

"You may be right," he said, finally. "But I have to give it a try. What

I need from all of you now are your best ideas and backup when and if I need it. Otherwise, I might just as well get back on that plane and fly back to Pittsburgh—and give up on the Bureau and everything else. And I really don't want to have to do that if I can help it."

Richard got up and went over to the window where he looked out on the City by the Bay. He stood there in thought then turned back to the group.

"When someone comes to me for counseling," he said. "I feel very humbled. After all, just because I have a few letters after my name doesn't make me the final arbiter of what is going on in someone else's life—and mind. I am continually weighing what the effect of my words will be—and even more importantly, what they *should* be."

Dave started to say something, but Richard held up his hand. "No, hear me out please.

"All my studies have taught me that the human condition is a grand and sometimes awesome combination of factors. Culture and environment play huge roles in an individual's life choices and simply how each one of us responds and reacts to every change and challenge we're given.

"What was it someone once said? What doesn't kill me makes me stronger?

"Well, that is a truism that is also very true. Our greatest successes may arise from the ashes of our very worst defeats. That is why I try to be cautious in advising my clients to take a particular path. I truly believe that the right path is not always what we think it is. I guess what I am trying to say here is, this is a challenge, one we have *chosen* to accept. Let's proceed with every tool we have at hand, our combined knowledge and experience and, most important of all, our will.

"Whatever comes of it, at least we can say we tried, for better or worse, to make a difference. We may learn new things about ourselves and our own strengths—not to mention our weaknesses in the process. Regardless of the outcome of this venture, it will influence our future outlooks. So, what do you say?

"Let's go forward and see where we end up, shall we? After all, what do we have to lose?"

* * * *

Later that evening, once Chip and Carl had gone to bed, Richard and Dave lingered on in the living room, enjoying one last cup of coffee, and continuing their discussion of the pros and cons concerning the case at hand.

Finally, Dave stretched and started to rise. He would be meeting with his California contact the next day and wanted to be fresh.

"Hold up a minute," Richard said. "There's something else I feel I ought to mention, if you don't mind."

"Sure, fire away," Dave said, sitting back down. "What's up?"

"Not much, really," his friend responded. "It's just that, we haven't really talked much about what happened—all that happened—on the *Nerissa*.

"I guess what I really want to know is, are you all right?"

Dave was silent a moment, gathering his thoughts.

"Hmm, well *that's* a leading question, 'what happened on the *Nerissa*'. Beyond changing my whole life? Is that what you mean?"

Richard waved his hand. "Now don't go all prickly on me, Dave," he said. "I'm your friend—at least I hope you consider me to be your friend. I'm concerned about you because I have seen very little evidence that you have gone through any kind of mourning process. You're allowed, you know—to have feelings, I mean."

"Yes, you are my friend," Dave said. "I acknowledge that wholeheartedly. God knows what I would have done without my friends, you and the others, through that whole process.

"But, as wise as you are, Richard, I think you will agree that we all grieve in different ways. I may not be as vocal as some, going about rending my clothes and wailing to the moon and all, but I have grieved for all that was lost—and I think I'm grieving still. It's just that I might not be showing it in the same way other people do."

"I understand, of course," Richard said. "And I agree. People show their grief in a hundred different ways. But what I *do* know—and here I claim superiority by virtue of my work—what I know is that there is a *process* called grieving which has recognized steps. I'm just wondering if you may have gotten stuck somewhere along the way between denial and acceptance.

"It's okay to be strong—admirable even," he continued. "But eventually we all have to own up to the fact that we're human beings. And, after all, that's not such a bad thing."

"I appreciate what you're trying to say, Richard, I truly do. But I honestly don't know any other way of dealing with what happened to me. I lost the two people who meant the most to me in the world—Conrad, my father figure, and Deb, the love of my life. And I still feel partially responsible for my loss because I was so damned enthusiastic about taking that trip. I thought that was going to be the start of a wonderful new life.

"Instead, it was the end of all in my life that meant anything to me. *That's* the reality I've been dealing with, Richard. It's the main reason I signed on with the FBI. I thought I might be able to do some good and at the same time I hoped I could come to terms with my losses by throwing myself into the work. I don't know any other way to deal with it."

"And I applaud you. At least you didn't hide your head under the covers and not come out for a year. And yes, some people do just that. And it is positive that you decided to take on a new challenge.

"All I'm saying is, sometimes we think we're dealing with something when we're actually just covering it up and running away from it. As your friend, I want to be sure that's not what you're really doing here. I understand that throwing yourself into this assignment takes your mind off other things. But I'm not so sure that ignoring those 'other things' completely is the answer either."

Dave shook his head. "So what *is* the answer then, Richard? Are you saying I *shouldn't* be doing this? If so, what do you suggest to take its place? I don't want to just crawl back to Pittsburgh with my tail between my legs and mope around there for the rest of my life."

"I'm not suggesting that at all." Richard got up and moved to the windows and looked out at the City he loved so much. "Look, a few years ago I believed I had found the love of *my* life. You know the story. God knows I've told it to anyone who would listen—too many times. She grew impatient with my nitpicking ways and eventually, through her choice, not mine, we parted company. I keep in contact with her, mainly to see how our mutual cat is doing." He laughed. "But we're over as a couple. And that was a huge loss for me. Not like the loss you suffered, of course. But like you, I found myself throwing myself into my work to forget.

"And that was successful, for a while. But I kept coming back to my sorrow. I couldn't let go of it. Finally I came to terms with the fact that what I was doing wasn't working. I went to see a therapist—a friend of mine whom I respected. His verdict was that I had not allowed myself to go through the standard grieving process over this lost relationship.

"I took his advice, attended a few sessions, read a few books—and did a hell of a lot of thinking about it all. The result is, I think I've come out of it a better person. I'm not healed completely, and I'm certainly not whole. But I am better! I can actually get through the day now without thinking about her and what we had—and what we lost.

"More importantly, I can do it without blaming myself, over and over, for all the mistakes I made. That's what I'm wondering about you, Dave.

"Have you forgiven yourself yet? If not, then maybe it's time to give it a try."

To his surprise, David Spaulding, the strong man who never showed his fear or his faults to anyone, broke down and cried. He cried his heart out right then and there in that apartment overlooking the City on the Bay.

Richard Black Wolf had come through again for him.

And now he knew he was finally ready to take on his next assignment.

FIVE

By the time the woman hit the streets in Miami, she had decided upon her back story. And when she began setting up shop in and around the Hispanic community and was asked about her background—as she knew she would be—she told her tale well enough, although without much emotion.

She was the only child, she said, of a single mother, a *cubana* who had fled Castro's regime in earlier years in search of a better life for herself

But making a living had been difficult in Miami's Little Havana. Wages were low and only menial jobs were available to uneducated immigrants like her mother.

By the time she was born her Mom had already been forced to live hand to mouth, moving from furnished room to furnished room and sometimes crashing with friends until the friendship ran out.

The mother continued in this pattern after her daughter was born, and the two of them spent many a sweltering night in fetid homeless shelters.

Sometimes, when the weather was mild enough, they slept in parks and even out on the beach.

Finally, after years of such hardship, her mother inevitably sickened and died in a Miami-Dade County Hospital Ward under Civil Indigent Status and was buried without further ceremony in an unmarked grave in the Potters' Field located in Kendall Indian Hammocks Park.

The grieving daughter had scattered a few wilted flowers over the dirt on her mother's final resting place as she contemplated an uncertain future.

But being of an enterprising nature, she soon found an attic room in an old boarding house in downtown Miami, where she struck a deal with the elderly landlady to stay there rent-free in exchange for cleaning the tenants' rooms and changing their beds once a week.

This part of her story was actually true. She had accomplished this feat the day after she flew in on a forged passport from Panama where she had left Larry's boat parked at his island compound after arranging for a local overseer and had paid him a year's wages in advance.

Her very first act upon moving in to the rooming house was to pry up a few boards in the tiny attic bedroom where she stashed her valuables and then threw a bright new area rug over the spot.

After all, there was no need to risk being robbed by someone unscrupulous.

She then began scouring the downtown streets for pick up jobs of any kind and quickly established a little concession of sorts, sweeping up the sidewalks in front of shops every morning, taking out the trash, and stocking backroom shelves.

She continued to work tirelessly from dawn to dusk, squirreling away her cash. She rarely paid for food, but became adept at snatching leftovers from customers' plates in the cafés where she swept up and washed dishes. She actually ate fairly well, since tourists often found the Cuban cuisine too spicy or foreign to their tastes.

One day a week she gave the boarding house tenants' rooms a onceover, vacuuming, swishing up the bathrooms, and changing the beds. She oversaw the laundry pickup and delivery, and made herself useful in other ways. Once in a while, someone left cash out unattended in the room, or she might find a dropped coin or a bill under the bed.

If anyone suspected her of taking anything, though, nothing was ever said about it.

She knew the keys to her freedom were certain kinds of papers and she set about to accumulate these as quickly and efficiently as possible.

First, and of utmost importance, she obtained a valid-appearing birth certificate which established her identity as one Carmen Ruiz, a United States citizen, born in Miami-Dade County, Florida, to a now deceased mother of Cuban descent and a father, presumed to be white, but unnamed and unknown.

This document was soon followed by a Drivers' License and Real ID, a Social Security card and, finally, a United States Passport. All of these items were available on the street if you knew where and whom to ask and—more importantly— if you could afford to pay for them.

She had no hesitation about using some of the precious cash she had gleaned during her travels and indeed, she considered the new identification papers a very necessary and valid investment of her resources.

Branching out, she added a High School GED and a series of certificates in various trades from the local Adult School. The crowning glory of these was a Certificate in Arson Detection, a subject of which she had some knowledge.

She avidly read the newspapers, both local and national. And she had great confidence that the evidence of her unusual training would come in handy in the very near future.

She wasn't certain just exactly *how* this might come about. But, as she had always done, she trusted her basic instincts—and they had never failed her yet.

In the meantime, she went over and over again her options for further escape and independence. First, she reasoned, it would be easy enough to reenter her native country as a returning citizen following an extended visit here on the East Coast of the United States.

She would have to use slightly altered documents to accomplish this of course. And this option was more than a little risky, given her back history. Who knew, after all, just what nefarious deeds of the past might come to light with even a cursory search of her original background?

It would be better by far, she concluded, to enter her native country at some distant point on the map—far away from the scene of the crime—so to speak.

And the easiest way to do that would be to go in as a fully-vested United States citizen, making full use of the various documents she now had in her possession.

Then, hopefully, there would be no trail of incriminating breadcrumbs leading back to her previous checkered existence and she could start over fresh, but in a completely familiar environment.

At least that was her plan for now.

Gradually, the woman now known as Carmen Ruiz began to dress a little more up-scale, scratching through the bins at the Goodwill for little-worn suits and blouses with good labels and hitting sales at the better stores. She started to lighten her hair a bit, and applied makeup to accentuate her unusually brilliant blue eyes.

Remarkably, given her back story, Carmen spoke grammatically correct English without an accent—although there was still an interesting little lift to her voice. But, oddly enough, given her prowess at disguise, she remained totally unaware of that anomaly in her speech pattern. And, since it wasn't an unattractive trait, it probably did not matter all that much in the long run.

She began dropping in at the local Florida State Employment Office every few days, just to check out the job listings. She never applied for any benefits, even though she might have qualified for them. Nor did she ever attempt to speak to any of the specialists there. Instead she used her visits to peruse the current offerings tacked up on the bulletin board in the glass-fronted cabinet in the main lobby of the building.

And then, one day, just as she had known it would be, the one notice she had been waiting to see was there. She waited patiently until the lobby had emptied out, quickly picked the lock on the cabinet, grabbed the announcement, and stuffed it in her bag.

She knew, without a doubt, that this particular notice had been meant for her alone. It was her ticket out of Florida and on to the next phase of her master plan.

She hailed a cab and took it directly from the downtown Employment

Office to a small nondescript storefront in Little Havana which had been recommended to her. She entered the jingling door and had a brief discussion with the receptionist at the front desk, who nodded knowingly.

"*Si, hay alquien...*there is someone..." The girl stepped away from her station and moved toward the back of the shop, motioning to Carmen to follow her. She pulled aside a curtain and gestured toward an attractive dark-haired woman in her mid-thirties seated at a table and going over what looked to be reports of some kind.

"*Aqui, es Blanca.*"

"¡*Es un nombre bonita!* ¿Como 'sta usted, Blanca?" Carmen said, using the respectful formal phrasing. "What a pretty name! How are you?"

"*Muy bien,*" was the reply. "*¿Y usted?*"

"*Muy bien, tambien.*"

She paused, as the receptionist left the area. "*Ahora, Puedes copiar esta foto?*" she said. "Can you fix my hair like the *dama* in this photo?"

She pulled out an 8" by 10" color portrait and laid it on the table. Blanca picked it up and studied it, turning it first one way then another.

"Yeah, sure. I can do it," Blanca said. "But I have to warn you—getting this exact color could cause some damage to your hair. I'll have to strip it first then dye it all over again."

"That's all right," Carmen said. "I don't care about that. But it has to look perfect for this one occasion. I have to look exactly like her."

Blanca hesitated, but just for a moment

"Okay," she said. "I'll do it, lady—just so long as you don't blame me afterwards for any damage."

The operator cleared the table of her paperwork and shoved it into a locker on the wall behind the table. She picked up the photograph gingerly in two fingers and walked back toward the rinse bowls.

"*Venga,*" she said. "No time like the present to get started. This is going to take me a while."

A day later, a young woman, carrying a large tote bag, stepped out of a taxi in front of an old brick building in downtown Miami. Her golden hair was expertly coifed. Her dark suit and tailored blouse were pristine and modish. Her eyes, behind the dark glasses, were hazel, not a brilliant blue. Her complexion was fair, befitting a blonde of Nordic descent. Her makeup had been expertly applied.

She entered and was directed to a separate area behind the counter where she offered an identification card which had originally belonged to Larry's daughter. She signed the register where indicated with the signature she had practiced to perfection and entered the password she had gleaned from Larry's papers in the wall safe on his boat.

The assistant nodded, led her inside the vault, took the duplicate key she offered and eventually brought her a long metal container, leaving her alone to go through it in privacy.

After examining every single thing in Larry's safety deposit box, she removed most of the items and stuffed them deep down inside her already bulging tote bag.

She called to the clerk, surrendered the box, thanking him graciously as she did so, and left the building. She returned to the cab which was still waiting for her at the front door and gave the driver her instructions. She refused his offer to put her tote bag in the trunk with her other luggage and held on to it tightly, next to her in the car.

All her planning had paid off. Her next stop would be Miami International Airport.

She was on her way to being free.

SIX

Burnt orange.

That was the color of Southern California during fire season—burnt orange hills covered with burnt orange brush, and fried to a crisp by a burnt orange sun.

And when the first seasonal fires began erupting, the sky was also tinged with a burnt orange pall.

And then, suddenly, in the midst of all this, the burnt orange tint morphed into a heavy black shroud, blanketing the upper slopes of Old Waterman Canyon.

The blaze was reported at 09:55 hours. The California Forestry Department's first-response team, luckily stationed not far off, reached the burn site at 10:03 and ordered the fire-retardant-spraying helicopters and water-bombing tanker planes out of San Bernardino International Airport (formerly Norton Air Force Base) to strafe the flames just minutes later.

And they had been very lucky this time. Everything had gone by the book so far. The quick reaction of the firefighters and the spotty nature of the wind had kept the flames from spreading beyond the hundred-acre mark.

When they found what they thought might be the point of origin a short time later, headquarters was contacted. The schedules were checked and management quickly plugged in one of the newcomers they had just hired to go out in the field and examine the site.

Her name was Carmen Ruiz. She was an arson specialist newly hired in from Miami, Florida and was still considered to be in training with the California Department of Forestry in Sacramento.

On this day, as soon as Carmen received her instructions and was given her travel vouchers, she hopped the local shuttle to Ontario International Airport. Once on the ground, she picked up a Land Rover, the rental car authorized for her by the Forest Service, and headed east on the I-10 Freeway, checking her in-dash GPS as she drove.

The city of San Bernardino was the seat of the largest county in the nation. It had once been an agricultural marvel, a beautiful lush valley full of orange groves and artesian wells, surrounded by the heavily forested mountains of the San Bernardino National Forest. It was also an extremely active hub of the Santa Fe Railroad and home to Norton Air Force Base during and after World War II.

But sadly, much of that shimmer had faded. The formerly lush valley was now full of blight and the closure of one source of jobs after another, first Kaiser Steel in nearby Fontana, followed by the Santa Fe Shops, and finally Norton Air Force Base, had negated all the pluses and left only minuses behind.

Still, as she drove through the area via the freeway, the woman now known as Carmen Ruiz could see that the graffiti-strewn landscape was mostly hidden away by native plantings and the blight of the city was equally invisible. In fact, the vista presented to random travelers seemed almost inviting at times.

She drove north on the 215, took the 210 where the freeways split, then exited toward the San Bernardino Mountains.

A few miles up into Waterman Canyon, she spotted CDF workers dowsing down the remaining hot spots on the blackened and still smoking slopes.

She pulled off on to the shoulder near a cluster of ash-covered, green-hued vehicles.

"Where's the point of origin?" she asked a man directing the mopping up effort as she showed him her ID.

."It looks to us like the fire must have started somewhere near there." He gestured to a spot about thirty feet further up the roadway.

She gathered her supplies, gloves, sample bags, and a camera, then taking her time, wandered slowly but steadily, all the while gauging the path of the flames as they had traveled up the slopes. She dodged a couple of departing trucks and tried to ignore the ever-pervasive stench of burning brush and flame-retardant chemicals.

After a while, it just became part of you.

A strong gust of wind rocked her, and she heard a shout somewhere up on the wall of the canyon. A tongue of flame suddenly flared toward the heavens, piercing the brown-edged sky with a fifty-foot-long spear of yellow-orange fire.

"Damned *Santa Ana!*" someone yelled.

El Aliento del Diablo, was what the *Méxicanos* called it—"The Devil's Breath."

Take one high pressure ridge planted squarely over the Western United States, add desert temperatures approaching 100+ degrees, stir in a clockwise motion of the atmosphere, bake for a day or two— add to that ten years of unrelenting drought—not to mention the devastating decimation of the forests through an infestation of bark beetles—and you had the perfect recipe for a typical Southern California disaster.

The devil winds could blow at any time of the year, of course, but they were even more dangerous when the brush had been baking for an entire summer under the unrelenting gaze of the sun. By then the chaparral, sage, and goldenrod and indeed all the miscellaneous grasses and foliage were just looking for an excuse to flare up.

And, truth to tell, fire had always been a necessary part of the ecology of the region. Many of the indigenous plants could not propagate their seeds without an occasional searing.

But man, that stupidest of all creatures, couldn't seem to stop building his homes on hillsides right in the midst of all that lovely, but quite flammable vegetation.

So everyone in the state, most especially the firefighters, had more than enough reason to dread the *Santa Ana* season. The winds made any first responder's task so much more dangerous. A blaze that might have been controllable under normal circumstances could suddenly, and without any warning, jump the fire lines, overwhelm the crews, and become a raging beast of a firestorm within minutes—seconds even.

But on this particular occasion, the devil's breath had died in mid-exhalation—and so had the fire it had helped generate.

Now it was time to get busy and investigate the true cause of the blaze—if at all possible. And that was Carmen's job.

A begrimed fireman was still working the site, watching for hot spots and making sure the embers didn't reignite, when she drove up the hill close to the designated point of origin.

"Have you got anything for me?" she asked him, looking around at the blackened terrain.

"We think it started up right about here," he said, gesturing. "There doesn't seem to be any doubt about it. We haven't been able to turn up the igniter, though. This one's a real puzzler. My name's Jim Brown, by the way. I'm pleased to make your acquaintance."

"Hi, *James* Brown," she said. "And do you make music in your spare time?"

He gave her a strange look. "Oh, I see," he said. "That's funny."

But he didn't look amused.

* * * *

They both got down and dirty, but still didn't spot anything. After an hour of mucking around on the blackened hillside underneath the unforgiving sun, they dug out a couple of bottles of reasonably cold water, and plopped down in the dirt in the shade of a fire truck.

"Looks like you caught this one just in time," she said, motioning to the crews still laboring up on the canyon wall. They had managed to squash the recent flare-up very quickly.

"Yeah, we were lucky all right," he said, taking a swig from his bottle. "If there had been a skosh more wind, though, we would have had some big problems."

"So, do *you* think this was set?"

He hesitated. "To tell you the truth, we haven't been able to find anything pointing to a natural cause. But we also can't find anything resembling an accelerator either. It's been a strange one."

"Have you been able to question any of the local inhabitants?"

"There's only one old house left up there—just around that bend." He gestured at the road. "It belongs to the Jones family. They've been in this area for years. There've been bad fires up here in the past, of course, but Jones claims he never even noticed when this one started—not until he smelled the smoke that is."

"Of course," she said rising. "Excuse me a just a moment."

Sitting there, looking about, she suddenly had spotted something odd back there in the brush along the highway, just about ten feet off the asphalt. After looking at what had caught her eye a little more closely, she gestured to her companion.

"What do you suppose this might be?" she asked, pointing to a six-inch-high mound of sand and soil. It came almost to a point at the top. "Have you ever seen anything like that before?"

"Hmm—now that you mention it, I hadn't even noticed that before," the man said. "It just looks like an old anthill or something like that to me."

He bent down beside her to examine the thing more closely.

"But see," she said. "It looks like somebody fabricated this. Look at it here. You can tell it's been pushed or poked into a shape."

Sure enough, it was obvious that someone had deliberately fashioned a small cone of rock and dirt, tamping it down firmly on all sides. Looking at it carefully, the vague impressions of fingers were quite visible.

She took numerous photographs of the unusual construct from all sides. Then with a pen, Carmen slowly began pulling away at the soil, starting at the top of the small mound, and stopping only when she encountered something hard and rigid planted right in the middle of the cone.

She carefully brushed the sand away, to reveal a small green glass vial plugged with a stopper. It looked like an old-fashioned perfume bottle, the kind your grandmother might have kept on her dressing table. The glass was unusual, almost wavy in texture, with a strange sheen.

Also, there was matter, something crumbly and black, lying across the bottom, way down inside. She was tempted to open it up and examine it, but decided it would be better to let the lab gurus deal with it. There was no way she was going to open this particular can of worms.

Carefully, she bagged the colored glass vial then took a few more minutes to pick through the rest of the mound. She found nothing else of any interest and decided to call it a day.

Even with this strange and provocative find, the fire crew still could not identify any specific cause for the blaze itself. It was agreed, in principle, that it was most likely a fire caused by arson, rather than natural causes. But they still couldn't prove that fact—especially without any evidence of an accelerant.

There were numerous tire tracks and footprints on either side of the access road that might well have belonged to the perp—but there were so many samples from so many different vehicles and individuals that it would be nearly impossible to narrow it down to just one person.

Nevertheless, she documented her notes with photos and casts—and that was all that could be done at the scene.

She headed back to her vehicle. She supposed that her job here was done. It would be up to more experienced investigators to make a further determination about the mysterious dirt cone.

In the meantime, some of the fire crews would be continuing their work well into the night, trying to make sure no sparks remained to ignite if the *Santa Ana* winds began to come up again.

There were plenty of bone dry slopes left to burn and tons of brownish-gold vegetation just waiting for the right combination of breeze and blaze.

Burnt orange.

Their whole world was tinted in burnt orange.

* * * *

But just as she was about to drive off down the hill and back to the Forestry headquarters, Jim, the firefighter she had worked with earlier in the day, came running after her.

"Hold up a minute there, Carmen—is it? A few of us have been given leave to go down and grab a bite to eat at one of the local diners. Would you like to join us?

"That was a pretty impressive find you made back there," he went on. "I'd kind of like to pursue that idea with you a little bit further. If you don't mind, that is."

She hesitated. Every instinct told her it would not be wise to have more than passing contact with anyone, including the locals. But the thought of talking shop about the fires had become intriguing to her. She realized she might be allowing herself to get too caught up in this pursuit of an unknown arsonist on the loose, running around the state and setting fire after fire.

But it was like reading a mystery novel and now she was curious to see how far the clues could take her.

"Why not?" she said although it was against her better judgment. She smiled at the man. "Shall I follow you in my car?"

"Sure, that's probably the easiest thing to do. It's only a mile or so down the main road out of the canyon. Just turn right at the first four-way light. I'll go a little slower and wait on the street there for you."

When they arrived at the strip mall housing the eatery, she pulled her Land Rover in to the parking space right next to his state truck.

"Thanks for inviting me along," she said. "I guess I am getting hungry after all."

They went inside where several of the other firefighters were already gathered around a big table in the corner. As they stepped through the door, some of the other customers clapped.

"Thank you for your service!" one of them called out.

"Welcome to Connie's" a large friendly woman swathed in an apron said, holding her hand out to Carmen. "We always have room for one more of California's finest!"

Carmen smiled back. "Just doing our jobs," she said. "But thank you for the kind thoughts."

Room was made for the two newcomers at the big table and Carmen settled in to additional welcomes and introductions.

"Chuck," said a baby-faced young man at the far end of the table, all smiles, and raising his coffee cup in her direction.

"Alejandro," said a short, dark–haired man seated next to him. He seemed more reticent than the others.

"*Yo soy Carmen*," she said, hoping to strike a bond with him.

He looked confused for a moment. "Oh," he said. "I'm Indian, not Hispanic."

"Sorry," she said. "I just thought…"

"Yeah," he said. "Most people think that. But I don't even know much of the Indian lingo. I was raised off res—the reservation—so I didn't get much exposure to it."

"What tribe, if I may ask?"

"San Manuel," he said, shortly. "They're the local bunch. They run most of the gaming around here."

"Hmm,' she said. "I've always been interested in the casinos and gaming. It seems to me it would be a fascinating world."

He looked at her with something like disdain. "It's all a make believe world," he said. "There's nothing real about it at all."

She was about to respond when the third person spoke up.

"Hi, I'm Wayne," he said. He was a handsome black man who looked to be in his forties. "I'm very pleased to meet you, Miss Carmen."

She waved back at them. "And I'm very happy to meet all of you, too."

"Coffee?" said the woman.

"That would be great," she said.

The guys settled down to small talk about departmental matters and back and forth questions about family members, how an ailing parent was doing, and when a new baby was expected. Jim, Wayne and Chuck were the most garrulous, trading quips back and forth about an unpopular boss and sympathizing with each other over money problems and possible upcoming pay cuts.

Alejandro laughed once in a while at the jokes, but he seemed much less forthcoming than the others about any personal issues he might have had. Most of the time, he just sat and stared pensively out the window.

At one point, Wayne mentioned he was hoping for some time off, one they were through with the mop up.

"I was thinking about booking one of those cruises down to Baja for me and the missus," he said. "There's one from San Diego to Ensenada that only takes a few days. I'd sure like to unwind and relax a little bit before the winds come up again."

Carmen had been feeling a little excluded. Looking for an opening, she spoke up without giving it much thought.

"I'd be cautious about signing up for a cruise," she said. "I've heard some pretty bad things about what can happen out there in the middle of the ocean with no backup."

"Oh," Wayne said. "What exactly have you heard? No casualties, I hope?"

All of a sudden she wondered if she had made a big mistake in entering in to the conversation so quickly.

"Uh, not really," she said hastily. "I've just heard that sometimes those cruises aren't very well organized and people don't get all the perks they're expecting—or have paid for."

Jim glancing her way noted that she seemed uncomfortable for some reason and tried to change the subject.

"Sorry, Carmen," he said. "These guys are like a bunch of old hens. We tend to get a bit gabby about our own problems and forget our manners in front of guests.

"By the way, I really meant what I said earlier about picking your brain, so to speak—on this whole arson situation. I mean, I really think you made a huge breakthrough back there on the fire site, finding that strange cone-like artifact. Now all we have to do is figure out how it plays in to the fire."

"It was just coincidence, I think," she said. "I kept my eyes open, that's all. There's no mystery to it. I just looked around and there it was. Remember though, we have no idea what the heck it is—or even if there is any connection between it and the fire."

"But you're the one who noticed there was something strange and out of place about it," Jim continued. "That's what was so special. And I've given it quite a bit of thought. I have no doubt at all that it does have something to do with the fire. We just have to decide what it means."

Just then Connie the owner came back to take their orders and they busied themselves making their choices. As she left, one of the customers at the counter across the aisle from their table turned around in his seat and spoke up.

"Hi," he said. "Sorry to interrupt, and I hope I'm not out of line, but I couldn't help overhearing your conversation about the Waterman fire. First of all, I want to thank you so much for all the work you've been doing. I'm not from around these parts, but I can see how devastating all this must be for the people living here."

Jim, the crew boss, answered for the group. "We appreciate any support from the community, especially from people like you who just happen to be passing through our neck of the woods.

"Actually," he grinned. "We can use all the support we can muster these days. We've got this Waterman Canyon fire pretty much under control right now—but I don't mind telling you, it's been a hell of a season—if you don't mind me saying so."

"Oh, I can see that," the stranger answered. "Look, Jim is it? I don't want to barge in or anything, but I'd really like to take my support a step further…"

"Thank you," Jim said. "We can't accept donations personally. But the Forest Service is always happy to receive support of all kinds. I can give you the address…"

"No, that's not what I meant, although I'd be more than happy to donate to the appropriate organization."

The man had turned all the way around on the swivel stool and was now facing them head on.

Chuck joined the conversation. "We've got an extra spot over here, sir. Why don't you come join us and tell us what you had in mind when you mentioned helping out. That is, if you don't mind sharing the space. We're a bit grimy these days."

Dave got up and moved over to the big table, coffee cup in hand. As he took the seat offered to him, he smiled at each of them in turn.

"Hello, and thanks for including me. I guess I should tell you my name and a little bit about me."

There was a general murmur of agreement.

"All right then, let me introduce myself properly. My name is David Spaulding, Dave to my friends. I'm a freelance journalist by occupation. I was born and raised in Pittsburgh, Pennsylvania and I've never been out here to California before. I'm *supposedly* enjoying the first vacation I've had in years."

He smiled and shook his head.

"But I have to tell you. Before I got here I had no idea about the extent of these fires and the destruction it is causing. I was planning to spend my time camping, hiking, and fishing in the mountains around the state. But that hasn't worked out very well for me—for obvious reasons."

He had found it extremely unnerving in the beginning that the Bureau had made the decision that he would use his real name and location of birth. Their reasoning had been simple. No one other than a few of his closest and trusted friends was even remotely aware of his new position and this assignment.

Because of that, it was deemed highly unlikely that his true purpose would be uncovered by the kind of perpetrator he would be attempting to track down. It was far easier, his bosses decided, to let him go by his legal name and background since it presented fewer chances of clumsy slipups.

The others all nodded to him and began to go around the table, one by one, introducing themselves all over again to the newcomer.

The only person at the table who had not yet looked him squarely in the face and welcomed him to the group was Carmen Ruiz.

On her part, she sat frozen in time. She had come to rigid attention the moment David turned around and began speaking to them, first because of the distinctive sound of his deep voice—and then by the confident announcement of his name, David Spaulding.

There could be no doubt in her mind. This was the very last person she had laid eyes on as the *Nerissa* slipped beneath the waves. She had looked deep into the face of David Spaulding at that final moment—just before the ship sank to the bottom of the ocean.

How in God's name had Spaulding tracked her all the way out here to California? After all she had gone through, including the chance meeting with Larry followed by all the subsequent plans she had put together so meticulously for her new life—was this going to be the moment of her undoing?

Her mind raced through all the possible scenarios she might be able to use to make her escape—to get away from her nemesis—for once and for all.

But then as the conversation continued, she began to realize that he did not act as if he recognized her at all. Thank God she had made enough of a change in her appearance and mannerisms that she now seemed to be invisible to him.

At least, that was the only thing that made any sense to her. Either that or he was a very good liar.

She remained quiet in her seat, trying frantically to remember if he had even heard her *real* voice while they were still on the ship—and what she might have said—or done—that would have etched her identity indelibly into his brain.

"I'm particularly interested in this theory of a serial arsonist going about the state and setting fires," Dave said. "If you are going to be making any further investigations with that part of it—well, I'm curious enough that I'd like to offer my assistance, in any way you folks think is feasible and acceptable."

Jim scratched his chin. "Well, you'd have to get the approval of the Forest Service, of course. But I don't see any objection on the face of it.

"How about it, Carmen," he added, turning to her. "Could you use some help? Maybe with those interrogations you wanted to follow up on with some of the locals? It sounds like this might be right down Mr. Spaulding's alley."

Dave glanced across at the woman sitting quietly on the other side of the table—and something struck him about her. She was mature, perhaps even near him in age, and very attractive, if not quite beautiful.

He tried to remember what Richard had told him about completing the grieving process and moving on with his life. What was it? You'll know immediately, the moment you meet that special person, that there is some sort of bond between you.

Don't turn away from it, Richard had urged him. *Welcome it with open arms—and make the most of it while you can.*

Carmen continued to look down into her cup as she stirred. Then she made a quick decision.

"Sure, why not?" she said, looking up with a smile. "Like Jim said, we would have to get permission from my boss at the local Forest Service office. But I don't have any problem with it. I promise you though, picking up random information from here, there, and everywhere isn't nearly as exciting as you might think it would be."

She raised her head then and looked him straight in the eye. They both felt a *déjà vu* effect from the encounter—but for entirely different reasons.

"Fine," he said, as soon as he regained control of his voice. "Where—and when—do you want to start?"

As she hesitated, he went on. "You know, when you said your name was Carmen, the very first thing I thought of was the term *karma*. Have you ever heard of it?"

"Oh, sure," she said. "I've heard of karma. I don't know too much about it, though. Doesn't it have something to do with reincarnation?"

"Yes," he said. "The Hindus believe that we all have lived past lives and can come back over and over again as different beings. If we committed an evil act in our past life, we must pay for it in our present existence. By the same token, if we did a good deed in the past, we are sure to reap the benefit in the present.

"And that is basically the concept of karma as nearly as I understand it," he added. "Karma can be good—or it can be bad karma. It all depends on what the soul has done in service of its own free will."

She sat silently, stunned by the implication of all that he had just said to her.

Before she could respond, Connie appeared tableside. "No charge for coffee for this table," she said cheerfully. "And all orders are half price for my special customers."

Dave held out the VISA assigned to him for this mission.

"No," he said, when she shook her head. "Charge the regular prices, and the table is on me this time. I insist," he added, as the others started to protest. "It's the least I can do to support the effort—and, Miss Connie, it's the least I can do to support what appears to me to be a most welcome public institution in this neck of the woods."

She shrugged, scooped up the card with a big smile and went off to run the ticket.

"Thank you, sir," Jim said. The others chimed in with their thanks as well. "You didn't have to do that, but your gesture is much appreciated."

"Oh, you're all very welcome," he said, signing the receipt Connie brought back, and adding a generous tip. "I'm just happy to be accepted as part of this group."

Jim stood. "Well," he said. "It's more than time for us to get back up there on the line, boys. We'll be mopping up for the next day or so, Dave. We have to make sure there aren't any more breakouts."

He turned to Carmen. "I guess we'll be seeing you around the area while you do your follow-ups. You've got my number, so be sure to call or text me if you need any further help or information from our end of things."

"Thanks a lot, Jim," she said, shaking his hand. "You do the same. Good luck to all of you and stay safe."

The others said their goodbyes as they filed out the door. Carmen and Dave continued to sit there for a moment or two longer finishing their coffee.

"So what's the next step, Ms. Ruiz," he said. "Shall I follow you down to the Forest Service Headquarters? Or would you rather wait until tomorrow and get a fresh start?"

She glanced at her watch. "Yes, let's do it now. I think the office is still open until five. We can go in and at the very least I can introduce you to my contact there. Hopefully we won't have any difficulty in getting his permission for you to shadow me for a few days."

"And then we can take the investigation as it goes," she added. "You may find yourself getting bored and decide you've had enough at some point. And that's all right, too. This arrangement won't be iron-clad, and no one—me in particular—is going to hold you to anything."

"Well, let's just play it by ear for the time being then," he said, holding the door open for her. "Now which car is yours? Is it that Land Rover over there? Okay, I guess I won't have any trouble following you. Lead the way."

* * * *

He plugged in his earpiece as they headed out of the restaurant parking lot and was able to make almost immediate contact with his handler in Sacramento. He quickly explained the situation and made the case that this might be a unique opportunity to tie in with the local investigation.

His supervisor agreed with his assessment and promised to notify the Forest Service headquarters in San Bernardino at once that they were to okay his involvement and participation without revealing why.

He thought about calling Richard also but decided to wait until later that evening, once he knew for sure he had been accepted and what his plans were going to be. Richard could then notify Carl and Chip who would soon be on assignment and busy conducting on-site investigations of their own in the other fire-torn areas of the state.

Dave followed Carmen's Land Rover into the large Forest Service complex located on Tippecanoe just west of the old Norton Air Force Base site (now designated as San Bernardino International Airport) where their retardant helicopters and water tankers were stationed.

Carmen being new to the area as well took several minutes to remember just which building she had been told to enter.

Eventually they finally found their way into a bustling office where a gray-haired man in his fifties immediately rose and welcomed them to his desk.

"Carmen Ruiz?" he said. "I'm Everett Hightower, head of this section. I'm very glad to meet you. I've been hearing some good things from the fire team about your efforts.

He turned and glanced with interest at Dave seated next to her. "And you are...?"

"David Spaulding," he rose and offered his hand. "As I explained to Ms. Ruiz, I'm a freelance journalist from Pennsylvania. I'm out here on vacation right now, but I've gotten caught up in this terrible fire situation. I see a story here, of course. But because I have quite a bit of experience in talking to people, getting their backgrounds and the like, I couldn't help but wonder if I might be of some assistance with the interview process, strictly on a volunteer basis. I'd just be doing my duty as a good citizen."

Hightower looked him in the eye. "I wish there were more people out there like you," he said. "It's amazing what can be accomplished if good people are willing to step up. I see no reason why we can make use of your services in just the manner you suggest.

"You would have to sign an agreement and a liability waiver, of course. And you also would need to agree that you will not hold yourself out as an employee of or representing the Forest Service in any way. If you have no problem with those legal requirements, I'll go ahead and get all the necessary paperwork drawn up right away for your signature and notarization."

"I have no reservations about anything you've suggested," Dave said. "The sooner we can get this done the better, I'd say. How about it, Carmen," he said, turning to her. "Do you think we're ready to get to work?"

"You bet we are," she said mustering an enthusiastic smile. "I think you and I are going to make a great team."

It took quite a while to free someone up to put the paperwork together, as well as find a notary in the area to come in and witness the signatures.

But several hours later Hightower called Carmen and Dave back in from the waiting area where they had spent the time going over strategy. He then reviewed all the necessary documents thoroughly with both of them. Dave carefully signed his name on the dotted line of each paper put in front of him, and the notary who had been called in attached his seal and signed them also.

At last, when everything had been signed, sealed, and delivered, Dave folded his copies and put them away in the small attaché case he was carrying for just such a purpose. Then the two new investigative partners rose and prepared to leave the building.

Everett Hightower took another moment to wish them good luck. He shook Dave's hand again and looking him straight in the eye, uttered the simple words, "Thank you for your service."

This moment was not lost on Carmen Ruiz.

There was something eerie about the way civilian David Spaulding had been so easily and earnestly accepted into the program with scarcely a question that had raised the hackles on the back of her neck.

She still could not get over the idea that this whole project was just some sort of scheme he had designed to entrap and expose her as an imposter?

Even though Spaulding still did not act as though he had recognized her from their brief encounter on the *Nerissa*, Carmen wasn't convinced that she was safely beyond discovery.

Time would tell, she supposed. As usual, she was going to have to keep all of her options open and have some sort of back-up plan in her tool-kit if she had any hope of remaining in the clear.

"Where are you staying," Dave asked her, as they left the building to return to their respective cars.

"I'm at the Hilton down on Hospitality Row," she answered automatically. There would be no hiding from him now.

"Great!" he said. "That's where I am, too. Why don't we go back there, maybe grab a bite to eat and make our plans for tomorrow."

"Fine," she said, resigned to her fate. "I'll see you there. We can meet in the restaurant."

He was already there and seated when she arrived. She had not seen him on the drive down and wondered if he had already scoped out a shorter route from one end of town to the other.

"We're a little early for dinner," he said, handing her a menu. "But it looks like they have some Early Bird specials. Will that be all right?"

"Sure," she said. "I'm not all that hungry anyway."

They placed their orders and while they were waiting for their drinks to be served, Dave began to outline how he thought they might begin their research.

"You said you were particularly interested in going back up into the Waterman Canyon site and interviewing any of the local residents who have been let back into the area. Did you have anyone in mind?"

"Yes," she said. "I certainly do. Jim told me he had talked to one of the families who have been living there for a number of years. This is the younger generation, of course. But he said the fellow he spoke with mentioned an earlier fire that had burned one of the nearby cabins down. I think he said he thought it was about ten years ago."

"Did he say why it stuck out to him? As a lead, I mean?"

"He just said it sounded like there might have been someone injured in the fire. He didn't have time to get much in the way of detail. But he thought it might be something we—I—might want to follow up on."

"Needle in a haystack," he said thoughtfully.

"What?" She looked at him puzzled. "What did you mean by that?"

"It's just that we're trying to find someone who may not even exist. And I'm beginning to think we are going to have to follow a whole lot of dead end leads before we get to the truth of the matter. If we even can discover what the truth really is."

She shook her head. "The truth, as you call it, may be something completely different from what we think it is going to be," she said. "I don't think we should go into this search looking for something specific. Sometimes it's best to let the knowable facts lead the way to the unknown.

"After all," she added. "A few hours ago we didn't even know each other and now we're partners. Did you think you would be sitting here this evening making plans for a man hunt?"

He laughed. "Now that you mention it…. But, I am curious by nature. I have been thinking about these fires quite a lot since I arrived here in California less than a week ago. This mess has ruined my vacation plans. But I'm not one to let an opportunity pass me by. I think there is a real story here. And now, thanks to you, I might be able to kill two birds with one stone, so to speak."

"You do speak in riddles, don't you?" she said. "It seems like I'm always asking what you mean."

"Well," he said thoughtfully. "I just meant that here I am, a journalist on vacation. And I find myself right in the middle of what might be the biggest story of my life. At the same time, I'm a sucker for mysteries. If there really is a phantom arsonist out there trying to burn the world down, what better mystery to try to solve?

"By the way," he continued, pulling a folded up sheet of paper out of his shirt pocket. "I've already done a little research of my own. Take a look at this and tell me what you think."

He handed her the notes he had taken during the session with Richard and the boys. She glanced over the list of statistics on serial arsonists.

"This is great," she said when she finished scanning the sheet. "It might enable us to narrow down our search a bit. I mean it looks like we might be able to ignore a sixty-year-old PhD for instance."

He laughed as he stuffed the paper back in his pocket. "Which is my point," he said. "About finding a needle in the haystack, I mean. The thing is, it could just as easily *be* that sixty-year-old college professor. There is absolutely no way we can eliminate anyone who seems even remotely suspicious."

She shook her head. "You are way ahead of me, David Spaulding. And, on that note, I think I'm ready to go up to my room. You're welcome to join me there for a nightcap, if you like. We could continue the discussion."

He glanced at her as he signed the check. He couldn't tell if she was making him a different sort of offer, but there was definitely some feeling of connection between them.

"Thanks," he said, easily. "But I think I'd better take a raincheck on your generous offer. I've got to…"

She looked up sharply. "You've got to…?"

He cursed himself. He had not meant to use those exact words. "I just meant I think I need to get some rest tonight—if we're going to make an early start tomorrow that is. It's been a pretty long day."

"Of course," she said. "That was silly of me. It's been a long day for both of us. I agree. Let's get some rest. It's liable to be an even longer day tomorrow."

He saw her to her room on the second floor then took the elevator up one floor to his room at the other end of the building.

And then he called Richard. He had a lot to tell his friend and on his end, Richard had information too. Carl had reported back on how his assignment was going. He was waiting to hear from Chip.

Now all they had to do was begin putting the pieces of the puzzle together.

* * * *

The next morning David and Carmen met bright and early at the coffee shop and began reviewing their strategy.

"Here's a map of the Canyon," Carmen said, smoothing it out on the tabletop. "The surviving houses and cabins are already designated with an X—and I've circled the Jones place in red. I think we should start there, and then try to interview as many of the other locals as we can find. Most of them should have been allowed to return back to their homes by now.

"Some of the places might not be in use by year round occupants," she added. "But from what the fire team said, many of them are. I'm hoping we'll be able to get some leads on potential candidates for this particular fire—or at the very least we may be able to eliminate most of the current residents."

"Sounds like you've done your homework," Dave said. He was still mulling over some of the issues he and Richard had discussed the evening before.

Not all of their conversation had been about the arsonist.

"But what do you really know about this woman?" Richard had asked after Dave had explained his new partnership and how it had come about. "Are there any warning signs or roadblocks that stand out to you?"

"You would ask me that," Dave said. "No. I can't see any specific problems with getting to know her a lot better than I do now. But all I *can* tell you is I am getting a very *uneasy* feeling when I'm around her. I've been out of circulation for so long—not to mention all the other traumatic things I've been through lately—that I'm having a hard time judging such things."

"Take it slow and easy then, my friend," cautioned Richard. "Use this assignment partnership to get to know her on a deeper level. But—and I can't believe I'm saying this after the discussion we had earlier this week—I don't think you should rush into a full-blown relationship with this woman too quickly. Even if the lady does seem to be willing, don't take her up on it all in a rush."

David scratched his head. "But that seems to be just the opposite of what you were telling me earlier—that I should be willing to open myself up to new relationships."

"I know I did," Richard said. "I just have this gut feeling that there might be more to this situation than we can see right now. If you have any reservations at all, like I said, my recommendation would be to take it slow."

So this morning, Dave was friendly enough, but kept their discussion all business. If Carmen noticed a difference in his attitude, she did not let on.

"And after we've done the interviews you've suggested," Dave continued. "I think we should try to hit one of the local libraries—one with newspapers going back at least a decade or so. There may be more information about the earlier fire—or fires—that might elaborate further on what the local residents remember."

Carmen finished her coffee and this time, she grabbed the check and signed it with a flourish

"No, I insist," she said when he started to protest. "It isn't fair for you to pay for all our meals. After all, *I'm* the one on an expense account."

Dave hesitated. He was on an expense account, too, of course. But maybe that was a little more information than his new partner needed to know right now.

"All right," he said. "You're the boss lady. I think we have a plan and I'm hoping we'll be able to turn up some interesting facts today."

"I think we already have turned up some interesting facts," she said, a little cryptically.

He looked at her and smiled. "You may be right about that," he said. "Time will tell."

SEVEN

"Jones," the man said. "My name is Terence Jones, but you can call me Terry. Please, come in and take a seat." He led the way into a quaint wood shingled cabin sitting back off the road in a copse of cedar trees.

"Can I offer you an iced tea?"

"No, thanks," Carmen said. "We just had breakfast."

"I have no idea," he went on, "…if I can tell you anything that might be of any help. But I'll certainly try."

"That's all we ask," she said, getting out a lined yellow pad and pen. "Just do the best you can to remember anything at all. It could be the slightest little thing that might help us shed some light on the origins of the fire."

She glanced over at Dave. "Do you have any questions, Dave?"

He looked down at his notes. "Yes," he said. "First of all, thank you, Mr. Jones, for taking the time to see us. As my colleague here has said, something that might seem inconsequential to you might have great significance when put together with other facts."

"Please call me Terry," the other man said again. "My father is Mr. Jones. Now I know you all want to know about the fire that happened here, in almost this exact same area, about ten years ago. I grew up here, and was living here with my parents at the time. But I was still in grammar school, so I'm not real clear on all the details. Of course I remember how terrible the fire was and how frightened everyone was. But I don't really know much of anything else about it.

"I'll try to remember as much as possible, though," he added. "Now what do you want to know about it?"

"That's all we ask, Terry," Dave said with a smile. "Just do your best. Now, you say the previous fire took place about ten years ago."

Terry nodded.

"And I believe you also told the fire crew chief who interviewed you earlier that you thought at least one of the other houses in the area had burned at the time. Do you recall who was living there? Or was the place empty?"

"I've thought about this quite a bit. What I remember the most is my folks saying 'Good riddance,' or something to that effect. I know that sounds terrible, but I think they had had problems with the old lady who lived there.

I assume they meant they were glad she wasn't going to be coming back there to live anymore."

"Do you remember what her name was?" Carmen spoke up. "Even a first name would be helpful."

"No. That's just the problem. I've thought and thought, and the only thing I can come up with is 'the old lady.' I'm not sure I ever knew her real name."

Dave glanced back down at his notes. "I think you also told the crew chief that you thought she might have been injured in the fire. Do you think that's the reason she didn't try to come back to the property to live?"

"Yes, I think I did say that. It's just an impression I have, but I have no clear knowledge of that. I wish my folks were still here. They both passed on a few years after that—in a car accident going around one of the curves on this road. It can be treacherous up here in bad weather."

"Sorry for your loss," Carmen said absently. Dave couldn't help but note her words seemed perfunctory and without any empathy.

"Well," she added, glancing at Dave. "Unless you have anything else..."

He thought about it a moment. "Yes," he said. "I do have one more question. Do you recall any other young men living in this area at the time of the first fire—a teenager for instance—someone a little older than you?"

Terry hesitated, thinking hard.

"Why yes, now that you mention it," he said. "There was one guy a little older than me. I'm not sure where he lived exactly, but I know my parents did not approve of him. I believe they had warned him off the property at some point. Although I'm not sure why they did that.

"And I recall now that they warned me, in no uncertain terms, that I was to have nothing to do with him. 'Turn around and go the other way if you run into him,' they said. I thought at the time that was a strange thing for them to say about a young boy. But I don't believe I ever saw him around these parts again after the fire.

"And I'm not sure where he lived and I have no idea what his name was."

Dave had been scribbling madly as Terry talked.

"Thank you very much," he said, closing his notebook with a slap. "You've been extremely helpful. Do you have any more questions?" he turned to Carmen.

"None that I can think of," she said. She was looking at him oddly as they rose to go

It seemed to her they had pretty much struck out with this particular interview. But Dave was acting as if he had found gold.

"Come on," he said to her, as they headed back to the car. "Let's go find that library. I think we have our first real lead."

* * * *

The spacious campus of California State University, San Bernardino was spread out along the foothills below the San Bernardino National Forest. The library there was open to the public during normal daytime hours. And, as Dave had determined from their Wikipedia entry, they had a fairly complete run of the local newspapers available to researchers.

After wending their way out of Waterman Canyon, Dave and Carmen found their way out University Parkway. Upon entering the campus parking lot they were directed to a kiosk where Dave was able to obtain a temporary parking permit near the library. Entering the modern five-story building, they went straight to the reference desk and were led to a viewing room.

"Here are the years that might be most helpful to you," the librarian in charge said, as she got them set up with a run of the *San Bernardino Daily Sun* for the previous ten years. "Let me know if you need any help or have any further questions."

They sat, side by side, peering into the viewer, as Dave slowly wound through the reel.

"It would be a whole lot easier if we had an exact date," Carmen fretted impatiently.

Seated next to her, Dave couldn't help but notice the haunting scent of her perfume. There was something familiar about it...

"There," she said urgently, pointing at the page in front of them. "That's it, isn't it?"

The headline was in large point and took up the whole top of the page:

DEADLY FIRE STRIKES IN WATERMAN CANYON

Beneath it, the sub header added:

An elderly woman met her death earlier yesterday when a wildfire fanned by Santa Ana winds burned her home to the ground

Dave drew a breath. He turned to the coin bypass set up for him by the librarian and quickly printed off all the pages involving the story. He sat back and began scanning through them, passing them off to Carmen as he finished.

He waited until she had read them all as well, then turned to her and said. "This looks very promising, I think. Now, we need to see if we can find out anything about that young boy in the area—the one Terry's parents warned him to avoid."

Dave continued reeling through the old issue, page by page, with no luck.

Suddenly he came to an abrupt stop on the issue dated about a week after the old lady's death.

"Look at this!" he said. Carmen bent closer to him to see where he was pointing.

He was becoming even more aware of her perfume now, and it was making him uncomfortable. Still, he managed to read aloud to her from a much smaller entry seemingly unconnected to the story about the wildfire.

"Local youth goes missing" announced the caption. It went on to describe a young man who was being fostered by his grandmother, but who had mysteriously disappeared from the area shortly following her sudden death. *"His present whereabouts are unknown,"* the story continued, *"and it is feared he may have come to some harm."*

The boy's grandmother's name was the same as that given for the woman who had died in the flames, although no connection was made to the recent wildfire in this story.

The boy had been known simply as "Charlie," and no surname for him was given.

"He would be in his twenties or thirties by now, I suppose," Dave said.

"I'm wondering," Carmen said thoughtfully. "This is a crazy idea, I know. But what if this Charlie is the same boy that Terry remembers his parents warning him about? After all, if he was living with the old lady nearby, maybe they had some sort of altercation with him on or about the property. What do you think?"

"I think you've hit the nail right on the head," Dave said, giving her hand a squeeze. An electric thrill raced through him at the touch of her skin. Combined with her almost overpowering scent, he was nearly overcome for a moment.

"Hit the nail on the head," Carmen thought. *Would this man never stop speaking in allegories?* She, too, had felt a sensation when their hands touched. But it was for far different reasons.

Dave printed off the additional page containing the story about Charlie and looked a little further for any more information about him. But the tiny snippet seemed to be all the news there was about the missing young man.

"Let's go," he said to Carmen as he gathered up their finds and paid the librarian for their copying costs. "I think we hit the jackpot today."

Carmen suggested they go immediately down to the Forest Service headquarters to let Everett Hightower know what about their discoveries.

'Not just yet," Dave said. "I need to make a few calls first."

Consulting the Internet from his phone, he entered an address and made a brief call before starting the car. He checked his GPS and headed out of the Cal State campus lot after turning in his parking permit

"Where are we going now?" Carmen asked, baffled by this flurry of activity.

"Oh, sorry," he said absently, watching for a street sign. "I thought we could head on downtown to the Hall of Records. I think we have time to check out the county birth and death records and the deed recordings for Waterman Canyon."

"Oh, I see," she said, settling back in her seat. She was more than a little irritated that Spaulding had taken it upon himself to organize all of their searches without at least talking it over with her first.

Still, it sounded as if he knew what he was doing, by suggesting they delve into the County records.

Maybe, she thought in sudden alarm, maybe he knew just a little *too* much. All this talk of birth and death records was unsettling to her. If he was so familiar with that kind of research, he might also be aware of how such documents could be manipulated by someone needing to establish a brand-new identity.

Carmen decided to keep her misgivings to herself for the time being. She would say nothing critical to Dave just yet. She must keep an eagle eye on him, though. And, after all, she could always complain to Hightower if he slipped up or made what could be interpreted as a huge error in judgment.

Maybe that way the David Spaulding she knew would be distracted enough not to dwell too much on how a person wanting to disappear might use the Vital Records system to their advantage.

They both remained quiet and lost in their own thoughts during the drive to the Hall of Records on Hospitality Row. If they found anything significant it would be easy enough to go straight from there to their hotel for dinner and leave the Forest Service notification for the next day.

The San Bernardino County Hall of Records building was set back off the main street behind a restaurant and a fairly large parking facility. It took Dave a few minutes to negotiate around the lot and find a vacant spot not too far from the entrance.

An armed guard stood attendance and both Dave and Carmen were required to surrender their bags for scanning before being allowed on site.

Dave couldn't help but notice that Carmen seemed somewhat nervous about letting the guard peruse the large tote she carried everywhere with her and he began to wonder just what it was she actually kept stored in the bag she refused to let out of her sight..

"Genealogy," Dave said, in answer to the guard's question about their purpose in entering the archives and, after a routine scan and search, they both were passed through into the building without incident.

Just inside the front door they were greeted by a seated receptionist who asked what records they needed to view.

"Birth and Death," Dave replied. "And perhaps land recordings afterwards."

The lady smiled knowingly. "Family tree research I'll bet," she said. "Go right through those doors," she pointed further down the hall. "Stop at the first available window. The clerk there will help you with your search."

"Thank you," Dave said, leading their way to the first door on the right. "Have a nice day," he called out as they left and the lady nodded at him.

The large service area they entered had multiple rows of folding chairs lined up facing a U-shaped bank of clerks behind long wooden counters. The seats were about half full of patrons waiting their turns and glancing back and forth from the slips of paper they were holding to giant overhead screens blinking with assignment numbers lined up with counter spaces. Every few minutes the screens would change to record the next batch of available slots.

"Whew," Carmen said. "It looks like they're really busy today. Maybe we should come back another time," she added hopefully.

"No," Dave said emphatically. "I think the lines are actually moving along pretty quickly. Let's go ahead and get signed in at least. If it ends up taking too much time we can always leave then. After all, we're right down the street from the Hilton. But I think we should give it a try anyway."

"You're the boss, I guess," Carmen said. She still wasn't happy about letting him make all these decisions without her input. But she couldn't find a reasonable argument against what he was proposing.

He glanced at her. "Look," he said. "I can just take you on to the hotel and drop you off if you're tired. I can come back and do this on my own."

She shook her head. There was no way she was going to lose control of her own investigation.

"No. I'm fine," she said. "Go ahead and get us signed in." She flopped down on one of the chairs and waved him away.

He hesitated a moment but then turned and walked to the sign-in counter and registered their names for the next available clerk. When he came back she continued to ignore him, checking some information on her phone. He started to ask her if she was all right but decided against it.

They sat there in uncomfortable silence for the next fifteen minutes before Dave spoke up. "There it is," he said. "We're at Counter #11. Let's go."

She stood, still silent, and followed him to the counter where he pulled out the paperwork from the library and asked the clerk if she could search for the old lady's death record on the specific date of the fire and, even more importantly, if it would be possible to search for the birth of a male child with the same surname during the fifteen years prior to that.

The clerk looked everything over. "I'll give it a try," she said. "I'm pretty sure I can find the woman's death record since you have an exact date for it. The unknown birth date of the child is a whole other issue. I might not be able to come up with anything there."

"Do what you can," Dave said. "Anything you find could be helpful."

They sat side by side at the counter. Dave couldn't help but notice that Carmen still remained stoically silent, apparently lost in her own thoughts. He made a few token efforts at light conversation, but she kept looking at her phone and acted as if she had trouble hearing what he saying over the buzz of voices around them.

Finally he gave up on it. He couldn't figure out what her problem was. Last night she had all but come on to him with her offer of a nightcap in her room. Today she was acting as if he didn't even exist.

He would run it all by Richard again tonight. Maybe he could figure out what was going on with this strange but tantalizing woman of mystery.

Just then the clerk reappeared at the window. "I think this is the death certificate you're looking for," she said. "It took me a while, but I think this is the one you wanted."

She handed him a document stamped with an official seal.

"You can look this over while I continue searching for the other record," she added. "I still have a few more years to get through."

"Thank you so much," Dave said. "I really appreciate the time you're taking with this."

"Oh, it's no problem," the woman said cheerfully. "If I wasn't looking for this one, I'd be chasing down something else. It's sort of fun really—like solving a mystery, don't you know?"

She left them to review what she had found and made her way back over to the files again to continue her search for the birth certificate.

"At least we were pretty sure this one would turn up," Dave said. Carmen was showing some interest, now that they actually had something concrete to review. "Of course, we still have no idea if the missing boy Charlie was actually born here," he continued

"So that's…"

"…like searching for a needle in a haystack," Carmen said with a grin, her first of the day. "Oh, well. At least we have something to show for our time. What's on the certificate? Any surprises?"

"Not really. It's pretty much what we already had. Although at least it's all confirmed—especially that surname. It's an unusual spelling, so I'm hoping that will help us turn up Charlie. If we don't find it here, then maybe it will be in one of the other records."

"Look," Carmen said. "It gives her birth date and parents' names as well. Now that's something we didn't have before. And look at that, will you?" She pointed a pink fingernail to one line in particular.

"You're right," Dave said. "I didn't pick up on that right away. But at least that's a good indicator of the relationship."

He nodded at her in approval. "That was a good spot, Carmen. Like I said, we make a pretty damn good team."

The item he was referring to was the line listing the parents of the deceased. There, in black and white, the old lady's father's given name was listed as "Charles."

"So, whether the boy actually was named for her father or not, she made sure he was called Charlie in his honor. That seems pretty obvious."

"Sure," Carmen said. "But who were *his* parents—the boy I mean? We still have no idea if he was using the same surname as the old lady."

"Hopefully, our clerk will be able to help us with that question. Look," he added. "Here she comes now—and she's holding some papers. Keep your fingers crossed."

"All right," the woman said. "This may or may not be what you're looking for. I did *not* find a birth certificate for a Charles with the surname you mention during your time frame. But I *did* run across this…"

She held out a new certificate to Dave. "At least it looks like a pretty good possibility to me."

Dave practically tore the paper out of her hand and began reading it avidly, with Carmen looking on over his shoulder.

At first he didn't see what she meant. It was a birth certificate all right, for a male child born a little less than fourteen years prior to the death of the supposed grandmother. The surname was *not* the same as hers as they had hoped. But after a moment or two of studying the document the crucial words leapt off the paper at him.

The child's *mother's* surname was the same as the grandmother's.

"It's the same spelling," Dave said. "This has to be the right one." He turned back to the clerk. "You have no idea what this means, ma'am. Thank you so much for putting in the extra effort to turn up this information. Now, what do I owe you—and may I purchase several extra copies?"

The lady assured him that she had been more than happy to give them a successful outcome to the search and yes—he could buy as many copies as he needed.

"I'm guessing this is going to be a nice little addition to your family tree," she said, beaming. "I always enjoy how excited people get when we can give them a successful search."

"Oh, yes," Dave assured her. "This is going to make a whole lot of people extremely happy."

Carmen nodded. *And if we have any luck at all*, she thought, *this particular bit of paper may make at least one individual very sad indeed.*

Armed with their two new pieces of information they decided to forego the property records search and head straight up to the Forest Service to deliver their most recent discoveries to Everett Hightower.

"Then I suggest we come back to the hotel for a good dinner and another early night," said Dave. "I think we've done enough damage for the day. I'm tired, and I'm sure you must be, too. What do you think?"

Oh, yeah, she thought sarcastically. *Now that we've finally turned up something useful you're asking my opinion.*

She didn't say anything like that to him, however, but merely nodded acquiescence and mumbled something about "That sounds great."

Dave couldn't quite decipher her words but decided not to make an issue over it. Maybe she was coming down with a cold. *Or maybe*, he suddenly thought, *maybe she is resentful about how much I've taken over what was supposed to be her investigation in the first place.*

If that was the case, he would have to remember to tone down his enthusiasm just a bit and let her take the lead tomorrow. Now that they had all this new information to go on, the ideas for further lines of enquiry should start coming fast and furious—from both of them.

Hightower just happened to be in his office and welcomed them with enthusiasm.

"So you have some news for me?" he said. "Good! I didn't expect you'd have much in the way of results this quickly. Come on in," he said. "Have a seat and show me what you've found."

Dave decided to sit back and let Carmen make the presentation this time, hoping that this small act of courtesy would serve to put her in a better frame of mind.

To his great surprise, however, she nodded at him.

"I'm going to let Dave fill you in on this, sir," she said to Hightower. "Most of these searches and their conclusions were all his idea and I think he will do a much better job than I can of explaining his reasoning to you."

If her statement surprised him, Everett Hightower didn't let on. Instead he turned to her assistant and with a broad smile encouraged Dave to begin.

"Go ahead, young man," he said. "I'm all ears. What have you found for us?"

Dave opened his case, pulled out the sheaf of papers gleaned from the past two days' researches, and began to elaborate on how he and Carmen had moved, from lead to lead, extrapolating where necessary, but always looking for hard facts where they could be discovered.

When he finished his presentation, Hightower sat back and regarded the pair with admiration.

"I think," he said finally. "No. I truly *believe* you two have pulled off a miracle of sorts here. Everything fits.

"Now, I'm not going to get out there and start trumpeting that we've found the serial arsonist for the whole State of California. No. I'm not going to do that, because I don't believe we can count on that here. But what I am going to say—and especially am I going to say it to your superiors," here he looked at Carmen, but she sensed he was also speaking in code to Dave as well. "What I intend to let them know is that I think you have found the most likely candidate for the arson fires which we know have taken place in Waterman Canyon, and maybe in nearby areas as well, for over ten years now. And that is a most welcome accomplishment.

"Congratulations, you two!" he added. "You have earned the everlasting gratitude of a very grateful State."

They talked a while longer, but Hightower, sensing their fatigue, encouraged them to go enjoy a good dinner. "Make sure it is on the State of California," he said. "…and get a good night's sleep.

"Then continue with the program you've started," he concluded. "I think your idea of going back and searching the property records is a good one. And I am absolutely certain you will both come up with other possibilities as well. That said, you've already earned your stripes today. Now get along with you, and good luck! And don't forget to contact me immediately if you need my advice or assistance—for anything."

Carmen could swear the older man had looked David Spaulding straight in the eye as he made his final point. But she tried to convince herself, without much success, that she still could be completely wrong about her suspicions of Dave's motives.

As they left the complex to head back for dinner she was fighting off a pounding headache and—not for the first time in her life—a genuine fear that her true identity was now—or shortly would be—on the line.

"It's a beautiful night, isn't it?" Dave said, as they entered the hotel restaurant and he signaled the waiter for a booth. "It's time for a bit of a celebration, I think."

EIGHT

Back at the hotel they enjoyed a nice dinner and Dave ordered a good bottle of wine to go with it. He relished every bite but he couldn't help noticing that Carmen was just picking at her food.

Finally he laid down his fork and looked across the table at her.

"What's the matter, Carmen?" he said. "You've seemed overly quiet to me today. I hope you're not coming down with the flu or something. Maybe we should take it easy tomorrow. We could just stay here and do some more planning. We don't need to go out in the field. What do you say?"

"Don't worry about me. I'm perfectly all right," she snapped. "Sorry," she added. "You're right. I'm just a bit off my game, I think. It'll pass."

He didn't say anything, but signaled for the waiter.

"Come on," he said after he signed the check. "Let's go up to your room. I can't have you getting sick on me."

When they got off the elevator on the second floor he marched her to her door, took her card key from her and opened it, then led her inside.

"Now sit down here and relax," he said, settling her on the sofa in the suite's living room. "Can I fix you anything before I go—a glass of wine— or how about a cup of hot chocolate?"

She smiled up at him and patted the seat next to her.

"Why don't we just sit here and chat for a little while. I don't want to talk shop, though. Let's just have an average everyday conversation—like normal people do."

It was an opening of sorts. Dave thought long and hard about all the implications of her words, and particularly did he think about the warnings Richard had been giving him about avoiding any deep entanglement with this woman.

"All right," he said. "But why don't you start. Tell me all about yourself—where you're from, your family and childhood—anything you like."

She sat forward, glaring at him.

"Why all the interest in *me*?" she said, her voice cracking a bit. "Why are you always so bloody damned curious about *my* life, *my* family—*my* background?"

He pulled away and looked at her in bewilderment. Who *was* this woman anyway? And why did he feel such an unsettling connection to her?

"Hey, Carmen," he said. "Take it easy. What's wrong with you? I'm not trying to cross-examine you. God no! I just hoped we could have a quiet evening of it. Sit back and relax, have another glass of wine maybe. And just have a normal conversation about something other than this damned case. Why do you think that's such a bad thing?"

She continued to sit there staring at him, wild-eyed, and trying desperately to regain her composure.

How could she have been so wrong about him? Was David Spaulding really here on vacation and just a volunteer trying to help her find the arsonist?

Still, for the life of her, she could not get past her conviction that it was something more than mere coincidence that had brought them face to face again. But how could he have known exactly where to find her—and how in God's name could he have known what name she was using now?

"Look," she said. "Maybe I'm sensitive because my story isn't all that glamorous—or unique—for that matter. I grew up dirt poor in Miami—Little Havana as a matter of fact. My mother was originally from Cuba, and she died under very difficult circumstances. We did not play at 'happy families' and I never knew who my father was. Is that 'normal' enough for you?

"Now," she went on, flopping back on the couch. "I have a splitting headache and I need to get some sleep. Why don't we do as you suggested earlier and make an early night of it. Call me when you're up and about in the morning. We can have breakfast here in my suite. I'll order in. And then we can decide what we're going to do next. Is that satisfactory with you?"

"Sure, of course it's satisfactory," he said, soothingly. "I'm very sorry about your headache. I didn't know how bad it was. I was just over excited I guess by all the good luck we had today and I was looking forward to continue the feeling.

"I'll call you in the morning," he added, "and sure—it would be very nice to have breakfast to ourselves here. Thanks for suggesting it."

So saying, he stood, gathered his brief case and headed for the door.

"Don't get up," he said. "I can see myself out."

A few minutes later, Dave was back in his own room and on his phone with Richard.

"The trouble is…" he said. "…I have absolutely no idea why her mood changed so abruptly. We were getting along fine most of yesterday. At least that's what I thought."

"Do you remember what you were doing just before you began noticing these changes in her behavior?" Richard asked.

"Nothing stands out—well, I guess that's not exactly true," Dave admitted. "And while we're at it, maybe I ought to give you my latest information on the arsonist first. Just so we don't confuse the issues."

"It sounds as if you may have found quite a bit on our suspected fire bug," Richard said. "I agree. Let's discuss your findings first. Then we can talk some more about your mysterious lady."

"You'd better grab a notebook then," Dave said. "We actually covered a lot of territory yesterday. We began with an interview with Terrence Jones who is one of the remaining year-round inhabitants of Waterman Canyon."

He heard a rustle as the other man moved to the conference table in his den and grabbed a yellow pad and pen.

"Shoot," Richard said. "I'm ready to take notes."

"I'll send the articles and legal documents to you as well, just as soon as we're through talking," Dave said. "But here's the gist of what Jones had to say."

He went line by line down his own lengthy notes, stopping now and then to make further conjectures. By the time he had finished with the Jones interview, Richard had already come to the same conclusion as they had.

There was something very wrong with Charlie.

"So," Dave concluded. "At that point, I suggested that we visit one of the local libraries to see if we could find any news articles about the fire and its aftermath."

"Good call," Richard said. "That's just what I would have done, too."

Dave paused. "You know," he said. "I'm beginning to remember that Carmen began acting peculiar right about then—when I first suggested searching the newspaper records."

"What do you mean, 'peculiar'?" Richard broke in. "What did she say?"

"I don't remember exactly," Dave paused to think. "I just recall that she argued about it at first, suggesting that we needed to take the interview notes in to Hightower and get his input about them first. But the University was so close—just a mile or so the other side of Waterman Canyon. So I more or less insisted it would be right on our way. That's when she started getting really quiet—while we were on our way to the library.

"I can't quite put my finger on it," Dave added. "All I know is that she just seemed more subdued than usual, is all."

"Go ahead. What happened next?"

"Well, once we got to the campus library and began looking at the newspaper records, she seemed all right again for a while. Oh, and, don't let me forget to tell you about the articles we found there. It's important to the case I think."

"We can talk about that later," Richard said. "Let's wait on that a bit. Right now I want you to focus on your observations about Carmen. I think that's important, too."

"All right," Dave said. He paused to pick up the thread of his tale.

"When we had completed our research and were preparing to leave the campus, I suggested..."

"Wait," Richard interrupted. "I know you too well, Dave. Did you 'suggest'—or did *you* make the decision to go elsewhere? Think hard about it now. This is crucial."

Dave did think hard about it. He thought a lot about it. Hadn't he *demanded* that they go directly to the Hall of Records Office instead of taking the newspaper articles to Hightower first as she wanted?

"I see what you mean," he responded. "You're probably right, of course. *I* made the decision about our next moves and I'm sure I refused to listen to her objections. She wanted to run everything by Hightower at the Forest Service office. I said no, it was more important that we follow up at the Hall of Records first.

"I even told her that if she didn't want to go with me I would take her straight back to the hotel and do the searches by myself."

"Uh huh," Richard said. "And how do you think that sat with the lady?"

There was a long silence while Dave took stock of the situation. He tried to remember just how he had phrased everything.

"I can't deny it," he said finally. "Richard, I took complete control of the investigation. And since I was driving my car, there was absolutely nothing she could do about it.

"I'm been a damn fool," he added lamely.

"Nevertheless," Richard said. "For the record, I think you were correct to follow up your library research at the records office. But it's clear that Carmen didn't agree with you. Where you went wrong in my opinion, was when you forgot it was *her* investigation—and, ultimately, it was her boss that needed to be pleased—and it was her job that was at stake.

"I get that you were operating with your FBI assignment mandate uppermost in your mind. But what you failed to take into account was that she knew nothing about what you were up to or what your motives were. For all she knew, you might have been just another male chauvinist trying to undermine a female's authority."

"Yes, I can see that now," Dave said. "Still, I couldn't help feeling that she overreacted. She could have just said to me, 'It's my case, and I'm calling the shots here,' and I would have backed off. Instead, she pouted and went silent—and then began acting very vindictive toward me.

"One minute I felt like she was propositioning me, sitting next to me with this intoxicating perfume nearly overpowering me, and the next..."

"Hold on, Dave," Richard broke in. "What about this perfume? Was that something new? You haven't mentioned it before. What do you mean, 'it was nearly overpowering' you?"

Dave tried to remember the exact sensation he had felt with her sitting so close beside him there in the library.

"Well," he said slowly. "It's a little hard to explain…"

"Try."

"All right, I'll give it a shot. At first it was just a suggestion of something, a whiff of fragrance. And Richard, I have to tell you, I honestly felt like I had smelled something similar to it at some time in the recent past. I just can't quite put my finger on it.

"Anyway," he continued. "…the longer we sat there side by side in those close quarters, the stronger that sensation became. At some point I honestly felt like I was going to pass out."

"And let me get this straight," Richard said. "Carmen became even more upset and belligerent with you when you insisted on going through the birth and death records?"

"Yes. That's exactly right," Dave agreed. "What does it mean, Richard? Do you see some sort of a pattern here that I'm missing?"

"Oh, yes," Richard said. "I see a pattern all right. And I don't like what I'm seeing one little bit. You've been saying right along that you can't get past the feeling that this woman seems familiar to you—that you may have met her in some other place or situation before. Am I right about that?"

"Yes," Dave admitted. "But I have no idea where or when. It's sort of a *déjà vu* sensation—if you get what I mean. I can't put my finger on it, but the feeling is certainly there."

"Well, let me give you something else to think about, Richard said. "What if you actually have met her somewhere before—and it was not exactly a happy situation? What if you *did* meet her before in a criminal circumstance?

"After all, it isn't as if you haven't been involved in many such situations during your law enforcement career. She may have changed her appearance—and her name—for good reason.

"What if this 'Carmen' person is actually someone else—a former criminal or suspect you tangled with in your previous job?"

Dave was silent for a moment. "I guess I haven't given it that much thought," he admitted.

"Look at it this way. If that was the case, and she had put time and effort into changing her appearance and her name, she might very well have used vital records *and* newspaper records to create her new persona. We both know that is possible. In fact, it's done every day. There's a whole industry out there that will produce any document you need—for a fee, of course.

"And," Richard went on. "If that is the case, even if *you* didn't recognize her, she most certainly would have recognized you immediately. And when you offered to help with her investigation, as innocent as it sounded, she most likely would have been suspicious of your motives."

"I never thought of any of this," Dave said. "But it certainly is a possibility. Now that you mention it, there have been occasions she came across to me as very uncomfortable at something I've said. And then there have been other times she acted that way after *she* was the one who made what seemed like an innocuous comment.

"I'm going to have to give this some more thought," he added. "But right now, I think I'd better call it a night. She suggested we make a fresh start again tomorrow after breakfast. In the meantime, I'll try to see if I can come up with any possibilities for a former identity for her."

"All right," Richard said. "But I don't mind telling you, I'm very uncomfortable with you continuing to work alone with her. Why don't you suggest going to Hightower in the morning for advice on your next searches. Maybe you can propose that he pull in some additional people to work with you. I don't like the idea of you gallivanting off to God knows where alone with her."

"Come on, Richard," Dave said with a little chuckle. "I think I can handle myself all right. After all, she's about half my size."

"You need to watch your back, my boy," said Richard. "You really don't want to test that theory."

At the end of their conversation, Dave sent over photographs of the documents they had gleaned from their searches to Richard's phone then prepared for bed.

But he had trouble falling asleep. He tossed and turned, going over and over in his mind every moment of the time he'd spent with Carmen Ruiz during the last week. Could Richard be right? Was she indeed someone from his past?

Finally, just as the clock numbers on his bedside table slid over to twelve midnight, David Spaulding fell into a restless doze filled with nameless shapes, like ghosts, flitting in and out of his fevered dreams.

And through it all, like a mantra, the sound of her voice echoed his words back to him like a fatal admonishment.

No matter how hard you try, you can never escape your karma.

* * * *

Richard Black Wolf had a lot to think about that night. As both counselor and liaison to his friends during their undercover assignments, he felt a deep responsibility, not only for their well-being, but he also wanted to see a successful outcome to their investigations.

He was making every effort to stay on top of their communications back and forth, and to relay whatever additional information he deemed necessary to their mutual search for the as-yet-unknown arsonist.

He had had lengthy discussions with Everett Hightower following the Forest Service agent's several meetings with Carmen and Dave. The latter had agreed to let Richard know when and if he heard from either of them about any issue or problem, and the anthropologist promised to return the favor.

Hightower was also monitoring Carl and Chip during their travels about the state and had also promised to keep an eye on their safety as well. And that was all Richard could do from his post at the Nob Hill apartment.

In the meantime, he was keeping all his computers and internet connections churning away 24/7. And he had already conducted numerous searches into the activities of suspected arsonists specifically within the State of California and even nearby states.

He had even begun pinpointing all the fires within the year that were known or even suspected to be caused by natural phenomena such as lightning strikes or random car backfires along roadways. In that way, he hoped to narrow down their investigations to only those conflagrations of a suspicious nature.

Even more importantly, he had urged Hightower to alert all of his field staff to be on the lookout for the telltale manmade sand cones like the one Carmen had discovered at the initial site in Waterman Canyon. Thus far, at least three more similar structures had been reported at sites other than San Bernardino County.

This was not good news. Initially, he had hoped they might be able to restrict their search for the elusive arsonist to a more limited area. But if this new suspect 'Charlie' was responsible for the telltale cones, they would need to broaden their investigations to take in the whole state.

That would be a Herculean task. In his heart of hearts, Richard had real doubts about the possibility of success. He hoped he was wrong, of course.

But, as he had reasoned before, it would be like looking for that proverbial needle in a haystack. All he could do on his end was watch and wait— and try to add what he could to the facts at their disposal.

He also was concerned about the safety and wellbeing of his charges. He wasn't all that worried about Chip and Carl. Their assignments had been fairly straightforward. They would be sent into certain of the burn areas which seemed most likely to have been arson-related. Once there, they were to maintain their covers as tourists from out-of-state, nose around a bit, strike up conversations with the locals in an assuming manner, and try to glean any possible crumb of information that might seem helpful to the case.

So long as they maintained the fiction that they were innocent onlookers with no particular axe to grind, they should be safe enough, he reasoned. They had both been instructed, over and over again, by both he and Dave about the dangers of going too far out on a limb with their questions or by revealing their official assignments.

Above all, they were warned not to go off alone anywhere with any possible suspect. They were to stay out in the public in groups of people— and they were to contact either Richard or Hightower at the very first sign of a problem.

David Spaulding, to Richard's mind, was a whole other story. The agent was, in his opinion, still vulnerable and grieving from the tremendous losses he had undergone on the cruise ship.

And, in spite of whatever counseling Richard had been able to offer his friend Dave seemed distant at times and unwilling to accept advice. He certainly was not going to listen to admonitions about maintaining his personal safety.

David Spaulding was a man on a mission. He would not hesitate, Richard knew, to dash headlong into the flames, if he thought it would secure the outcome they were all seeking.

The second assignment, by chance, had come to Chip.Lutz. Not long after the Waterman Canyon fire was secured, a new blaze had broken out in the mountains just to the north and west of the canyon. It was close enough in distance that an immediate decision was made to send someone in to reconnoiter the scene and try and determine if they might be dealing with the same cause.

Chip's visit to Everett Hightower went well. He received his instructions and vouchers, and went over the maps carefully before heading out.

Once he had left the office, though, Hightower placed a call to Richard. "Has he gone?"

"Yes," Hightower said. "But I don't mind telling you, I hated to see the guy heading out by himself like that. He seems like a sharp enough fellow, dedicated and highly-motivated and all that, but…"

"If you have any doubts about his judgment, Ev," Richard said, a tiny stab of apprehension hitting close to his heart. "I mean, I don't have a problem with pulling him back. Maybe Carl Frick would have been a better choice for this assignment."

"No." There was a brief silence while Hightower gathered his thoughts. "I mean I think I would have misgivings for either of them in this situation."

"How do you mean, 'this situation'?"

"It's the location I'm actually talking about. It's not in any kind of highly populated setting. There's a large camp ground and an old riding stable nearby. But they're both no longer being used—and they're right adjacent to the worst of the fire area. So the investigator given this task will be showing up unannounced at an extremely remote site. The tourist cover story isn't going to fly."

"Has he headed out already?" Richard was poised to hit the button for Chip's phone to order him off the assignment immediately.

"Yes, he left the office a while ago. And I *did* warn him, Richard. I think he's smart enough to pull out if he thinks it's necessary."

"Okay. Now where exactly is this place?" Richard had pulled out his trusty pad by now and was prepared to take notes.

"Camp Seely is an old closed down family resort located in an unincorporated area of the San Bernardino Mountains known as Cedar Pines Park. It's just a little northwest of Crestline. The Waterman Canyon site is to the east and at a much lower elevation in the foothills. The two sites are not that close.

"We're talking remote and unsettled mountain territory here, Richard," Hightower continued. "That's the main reason I'm concerned. The resort is not near any real town so there's no local hangout where people congregate, like a diner or that sort of thing. I believe most of the few year-round occupants have gotten their animals moved out and the whole area has been under voluntary evacuation orders until they make a decision about containment later on today."

"I see," Richard said. "So when Chip shows up at this remote camp site his cover story about just being a tourist taking in the sights isn't going to be very believable."

"You get my point exactly. It's really your call, Richard. You know the man much better than I do. Do you think Chip can handle this assignment without exposing himself to danger?"

Richard had been pulling up maps of the area as they spoke. Yes, there it was. He could see what Hightower was talking about.

"What about Lake Silverwood?" he said. "Couldn't he just go in from that direction, claim he got lost and is looking for directions for a way out?"

"Of course. And that's exactly what I would have done. Although the way in via that route could be shut off by now too. We may be looking for trouble where there is none. He might not be able to get in to that area under any circumstances, if the authorities have closed all the roads down. There are only a couple of ways in and out of there in any case."

"Where exactly is the main site of the Camp Seely fire right now? Do they have any projected time of containment?"

"Not yet," Hightower said. "Although I don't think it has burned up very much acreage yet. They've strafed it with flame deterrent, but I'm not sure if the tankers are up and flying yet. They may be sending them out from the Adelanto station. Sometimes wind can be a factor.

"I'll be keeping an eye on all that throughout the night though," he added. "I don't plan to leave the office while this is all going down."

"You have my sympathies," Richard said. "I suspect you're right. Chip may not be able to get through to Camp Seely in any case. If so, and he contacts either one of us, we can instruct him to shut down his operations and come back in."

"All right," Hightower agreed. "That's what we'll do. In the meantime, though, if I learn of any further developments with the fire I'll let you know immediately—and you do the same if you hear from Chip."

Agreed on a plan of action, the two said their goodbyes and hung up. Richard sat staring out at the city of San Francisco for a very long time.

Sometimes the burden on those who watch and wait is almost too much to bear.

NINE

Chip Lutz stopped off at a bustling little diner at the crest of Cajon Pass and ordered the blue plate special. When Lucy the waitress brought his coffee he gestured out the window.

"That looks like a lot of smoke over there," he said. "Is that a fire burning on the other side of Lake Silverwood? Have you heard anything about where it is exactly? I was hoping to stop off at the campground on the Lake tonight and get in a little fishing tomorrow."

"Oh, that fire's way over there by Cedar Pines Park," she said. "I'm not sure if they're letting people in and out of the Silverwood Recreation area though.

"I can ask around if you like," she added. "There's usually a couple of the law enforcement guys in here about this time of day—and they do like to gossip." She laughed.

"Thanks, Lucy" he said. "I'd appreciate that a whole lot. No point in driving all the way over there if I won't be able to get in."

Half an hour later, Chip's thermos was filled with steaming hot coffee and a sound tip was nestled in Lucy's pocket. He pulled out of the graveled lot and headed straight out Route 15 towards the Highway 138 turn off to Lake Silverwood.

He stayed on 138 until he was greeted by a group of police and Highway Patrol cars blocking off access to the Lake itself, just as Lucy had warned him it might be.

He rolled down his window, "Good day, officer," he said politely. "Looks like you have some sort of trouble up ahead."

"Good afternoon, sir," was the reply. "Are you a local resident? Or do you have other business in the area? We're suggesting non-residents or casual visitors steer clear of the Lake for the time being. We're dealing with a pretty serious fire further up into the hills and we don't want any civilians exposed to danger."

He took a shot at it.

"Yes," he said. "As a matter of fact I do have official business having to do with the fire scene."

Chip was aware he was violating everything he had been warned *not* to do—by both Richard and Hightower. But something was telling him this might be an important moment for their search. And above all else, his greatest desire was to prove himself of value to Dave—and to their mutual investigation.

So he pulled out his government identification which he had been admonished not to show to anyone—unless he was faced with an extreme emergency—and handed it over to the officer on duty.

"So," the man said. "According to this, it looks as if you've been assigned to help investigate the origins of this fire?"

"Yes," he said. "That's exactly what I'm here to do." That wasn't exactly a lie.

"Very well, sir. Your paperwork seems to be in order. Have a safe and successful journey."

The officer saluted him and stood back to let him through, motioning to the other troopers that he had passed muster.

So Chip Lutz, contrary to all the warnings he had been given, turned on to Highway 138 and began making his way toward the Lake Silverwood Recreation Area. From there, with any luck, he would be allowed to continue on toward the Camp Seely fire site just the other side of Cedar Pines Park.

He sincerely hoped his decision to go against orders would not blow up in his face. In the meantime, he would keep his eyes and ears open and find out as much as he could about the origins of this particular fire.

After all, wasn't that what he was here to do? Chip desperately wanted to prove himself the equal of his colleagues. Here was his golden opportunity. He only hoped he would be up to the task.

The Lake Silverwood Recreation area featured a large reservoir dammed off to capture much needed water from a tributary of the Mojave River. Its scenic northern shoreline ran for approximately 13 miles up into the western foothills of the San Bernardino Mountains.

During the summer months it was a popular spot for boating, swimming, and fishing enthusiasts. Now, as Chip drew near the lake itself, he could see that people were being turned away in droves from the campground and an ominous cloud of black smoke hung over the trees into the distance.

"We're asking people to stay away," the trooper explained when Chip presented his credentials. "We think they're getting close to containment, now that they've been able to bring in the tankers." He gestured at a 747 which had just dropped a load of water and was circling to return to base.

"But we really don't need civilians up in that area while we're still mopping up."

"I understand," Chip said. "I'll try to stay out of the way of the crews. If it's all right though, I would like to start looking over any areas that have been cleared."

The trooper stared at him for a moment, looked back at the paperwork, then handed it back with a smile.

"Well," he said. "I don't see any harm in that. Just be careful, though. Those fires can be pretty tricky. I suppose you know that though."

"Thank you, sir," Chip said. "I'll keep my eyes open."

He had no idea what he was going to do when he reached the original fire site just a little north of Cedar Pines Park but decided he would just wander around a bit, get the lay of the land, and keep his eyes open for anything that looked odd or suspicious.

He turned off the road leading in to old Camp Seely and parked in a spot that seemed safely out of the way of entering and leaving vehicles. Without giving it too much thought, he disconnected the car's tracking device. The last thing he wanted was someone coming out to look for him and undermining any progress he was making in the investigation.

He gathered his gear bag of tools, notebook and camera then made his way on foot in to the campground itself.

The place looked like a war zone.

There had been at least four local fire crews assigned to this blaze, and several volunteer hot shots from out of state. A bivouac of sorts had been set up in an open field between the tumbledown camp buildings and the deserted corrals which were all that were left of the nearby riding stable. Any animals which had been on site had long ago been transported out to safety.

He stood and looked about, getting his bearings, and thinking about his cover story. Eventually a fireman spotted him and gestured him over.

"You're not part of the fire team, are you," the man said. "This is a restricted area and I'm afraid I'm going to have to ask you to leave. It's not safe here."

Chip pulled out his credentials again and handed them over. The man took them gingerly between his fingers, trying not to smudge them.

He perused them carefully, looking back and forth at Chip a couple of times, then handed them back.

"All right," he said. "So you're authorized to do an investigation on the fire *site*. But this is still an active scene. We could have very dangerous flare ups at any minute. The winds are unreliable, and we've still got acres of ground to cover to make sure there aren't any embers or sparks remaining.

"It will be days before we can declare this area safe. I don't have the authority to order you away. But I do want to make it clear that I will not take any of my men off the line in order to escort you around."

"I agree. I'm not here to make trouble. But at the same time, I'm on special assignment to search for information about the causes of these fires while the evidence is still fresh. The longer the scene sits, the more likely we'll miss something important.

"And I promise you," he added. "I will make every effort not to get in the way or cause difficulties for your crews."

"All right," the man said. "I'll have to take you at your word. My name is Jim, by the way. Let me take you over and introduce you to my crew. We can give you an idea of the scope and range of the fire and just where we are in terms of getting it under control. It's possible one of them may have noticed something out of the ordinary."

"Thank you. My name is Chip. I appreciate anything you and your men can tell me. And I do promise not to get in the way."

He followed Jim over to a handful of men gathered on one of the old cottage porches. Some were seated and two were snoozing on makeshift bedrolls.

"This here is Chip," Jim announced. "Give him whatever information you can about the fire and anything odd you may have noticed. He's been sent by the government to try and find a cause."

He shook Chip's hand. "I've got to get back to the planning station," he said. "We've just got notice we may be called off this fire and reassigned shortly. A blaze up in the northern part of the state that was nearly contained has reignited—and they may be pulling in everyone from all over the state on that one.

"Just remember what I told you. Try to stay out of the way—and above all—stay safe."

Chip would have cause to remember Jim's words in the near future.

He stood there awkwardly for a moment or two. His gear bag weighed heavily on his shoulder and he almost wished he had left it in the car. Still, if he found anything of note he wanted to be prepared to make a record of it on the spot.

Jim's men took in the newcomer. One yawned and went back to looking over some items in his pack. Another pointedly turned away and ignored Chip completely.

Finally one spoke up. "So what exactly is it you're looking for? And how do you think we can help you?" His tone was neither friendly nor hostile, but Chip hardly felt welcome.

"Hi," he said, hoping to break the ice a bit. "I realize you have far more important things to do right now than entertain me. But I really am here on an important task of my own."

The one who had spoken stood up and offered his hand. "Sorry we seem like such a lackadaisical bunch, Chip. We've been on the fire lines for a number of days now, here and other places. We're pretty much worn out.

"My name is Chuck, by the way," he added. "Tell us what you need and I promise we'll let you know right away if we can help. After that I'm afraid, you're pretty much going to have to fend for yourself."

"Agreed," Chip said, relieved to at least get the much response. "Here, let me explain what I'm doing and how you might help me…"

He pulled out his map of the area and began to describe the specific things he was investigate, including the point of origin if known yet, any spotting of the telltale manmade cones, and scuttlebutt about odd or suspicious characters known to have been in the area at the time the fire began.

Gradually, the others gathered about and began to take an interest, introduced themselves one by one and offered what bits of information they had gleaned over the past twenty-four hours.

As they talked, they told a little about themselves, where they were from originally, how they had gotten involved in firefighting, and just how hopeless their jobs seemed at times.

"I'm from Pittsburgh myself," Chip said. "This is my first assignment on the West Coast. I've never been to California before and I really wish it wasn't under these circumstances. It's a beautiful place. I'd like to come back and visit when I can actually do some sight-seeing."

There was an awkward silence. Then one of the men spoke up.

"That's funny," he said. "We ran in to another fellow from Pittsburgh just the other day. It was down on the Waterman fire. He wasn't with the government—at least that's what he said. But he was awfully interested in the fire. Pushed his way right in, near as I can remember. You wouldn't have heard of him I suppose—his name was David something…"

"Spaulding," one of the other men said. "His name was David Spaulding and he was from Pittsburgh, just like you."

Chip felt frozen in time. This was why he had been warned not to share too much detail with strangers. He tried to think how to respond without blowing Dave's cover and yet not sound as if he was lying.

"Really?" he said, hoping he sounded convincing. "No, can't say that I've ever heard of him. Well, I guess it's a small world, isn't it? I'll have to watch out for him if he's still in the area. It sounds as if we'd have a lot in common."

He reached back down for his map. "So, you think the point of origin may be up in this area? Would it be safe enough for me to hike up in there and take a look?"

"Well," Chuck said. "It's a bit of a walk, but people go up there all the time. It's called Heart Rock, a natural landmark of sorts and a real pretty spot. The trail isn't bad and it's only about a mile, I think."

"Great," Chip said, relieved. The awkward moment seemed to have passed. "If one of you can show me where the trail starts, I can manage on my own. I don't want to take any of you away from your duties."

"I'll take him." The man who stepped forward had not offered much during the previous conversation, but seemed willing enough to act as Chip's guide. "It's not far from here and the trail up there is well-marked."

"Thank you all," Chip said. "Thanks for the help. I really appreciate you taking the time. I'll try to stay out of your way

"Just be careful up there on your own. We won't know if you get into trouble, so we won't be able to help."

"No, I'm just going to go up and have a look around. I'll be careful."

This was his second warning he realized. Would the third time be the charm?

His guide waited patiently as he checked his gear one more time and got it slung around his neck and shoulder.

"All right," he said. "I'm ready. Lead away."

"It's an easy walk," was the answer. "Just follow me."

When they reached the head of the actual trail, Chip was relieved. The path was wide, relatively clear, and the walk was easy.

"It's only a mile back there you say?"

"Yes." We should be there in twenty minutes or so. Just let me know if you need to take a breather."

So saying, his companion swung ahead maintaining a steady pace. Chip had no trouble keeping up, but wished he had more of a chance to get the guy's opinion on places to look for clues. He tried to keep his eyes open for anything suspicious as they walked but found he was paying more attention to where to place his feet.

"Here we are," the man said, standing back so Chip could see. "This is where we think the point of origin may have been."

The guide gestured at a darkened area in the grass alongside the trail. The telltale debris left by the raging fire spread off to one side of a wooded area and down through the canyon to the west. There was a clear path of trees swept clean and undergrowth and brush which had been devoured by the beast.

"And here," he stepped to the other side of the path, "This is why this spot is so popular."

They were standing at the very edge of a steep precipice overlooking a massive rock face. Chip eased to the rim and peered over. Directly below him were several stone bowl-like caverns containing water.

The largest of them was in the exact shape of a heart. The effect was stunning.

"Beautiful," he said. "I can see what you mean."

He turned back to say something else, but his guide was already half way up the trail.

"Sorry," he called out. "I've got to get back. They're shipping my crew out to a different location. You should be able to find your way to the camp all right. Just follow the trail."

"Sure," Chip said, although the man was almost out of earshot. "Thanks for your help."

He turned back to the caverns and stood there for a little while, taking in the beauty of the unusual formation. He had never seen anything quite like this before and wanted to enjoy it before getting to work.

Then he thought of his camera. He really should take a picture of Heart Rock to commemorate the occasion. At least it would help document the location of the point of the fire's origin.

He tried to slip the heavy strap up and over his head only to get it stuck on his shirt collar.

"Damn," he said, tugging at the strap to pull it loose.

"You'd better be careful there, 'Pittsburgh'. These rocks can be mighty treacherous."

The whispered words were aimed right at the back of his neck. He started to wheel around but before he could do so his gear strap was pulled taut against his throat and he found himself unable to move.

He lost his footing and was either pushed or began falling forward, in slow motion it seemed, over and down the steep cliff and straight into the black waters of the Heart Rock cavern.

The last thing Chip remembered, before he lost consciousness was the advice Richard Black Wolf had given him.

Whatever else you do, never reveal who you are or what you are up to.

* * * *

Chip Lutz realized immediately how extraordinarily fortunate he had been. Several inches, one way or the other, and he would have landed either directly on the hard rock formations, or at least grazed one of them. He could have been gravely injured or even killed instantly.

He understood that as he plunged directly into the little pool formed by the Heart Rock basin. He was also lucky that there had been sufficient rain throughout the dry season so that the cavern actually contained water.

In fact, the depth of the water was sufficient to cushion his fall from the precipice above and, at the same time, shallow enough that he could reach the rim of the basin and, with some effort, pull himself up and over onto the mossy bank surrounding the Heart Rock cavern.

He lay there, panting like a puppy dog, for several minutes. Then he pulled himself up to a sitting position and took stock of his situation and tried to decide what his next move should be.

Clearly his would-be assailant had been counting either on his instantaneous death or an injury serious enough to render him helpless long enough that he might die before help could get to him.

His main concern was whether or not the attacker was still nearby or might come back to check on his outcome. If so, he would be in double jeopardy once the assailant knew he had survived.

No. He was now reasonably certain he knew the identity of the arsonist. If he was correct, the man was now or soon would be on his way to the new fire location and would not have an opportunity to come back and make sure Chip hadn't survived.

He glanced around. Even though he had fallen down from the trail head above the precipice, he soon realized there was a second trail leading out from this vantage of the caverns, probably to accommodate tourists who came in to swim in the pools.

He felt about to make certain he hadn't suffered any broken bones, sprains, or other obvious injuries. Then slowly and carefully, he pulled himself to his feet, steadying himself against a nearby tree. All seemed well. Beyond feeling a bit woozy and winded from his exertions to lift himself out of the water, he did not detect any lasting effect from his tumble. He was soaking wet, and his watch and phone were no longer functioning, but otherwise he seemed to be in one piece.

He pulled off his boots, one by one, and emptied them of the brackish water. Then, taking a deep breath, and keeping an eye out for anyone or anything suspicious, Chip set out on the trail back to Camp Seely.

He wondered who among the firefighting crews would be left at the camp—and more importantly, what was he going to tell them? The hike was only a mile or so, and as he sloshed along, he began to admit to himself that he was scared out of his wits.

What if he was completely wrong about the identity of his assailant? After all, he didn't actually see the culprit. And the whispered voice could have belonged to anyone. The further he walked the more apprehensive he became.

He drew up short at a turn in the path which led directly into the area between the campground and the old riding stables. He was still shielded by the brush and the few remaining trees at the edge of the trail.

What if he skirted the campground altogether? If he went up into the woods a bit on the other side of the corrals, he might be able to circle around to the access road unseen. If his car was still parked there, he could make his escape back to the highway without having to report the attack to anyone still left in the camp. He doubted that the authorities were checking leaving traffic. They would only be stopping drivers coming in to the area.

Carefully he edged into the brush, trying not to make any noise and hoping his movements would not set off any telltale quivering amongst the leaves. His boots were still sloshing a bit, so he stepped carefully and slowly, hoping to avoid disclosing his whereabouts.

But as he leaned forward to judge his position, he caught a motion off to one side. He stopped cold, holding his breath. Was that a person, rummaging around in the undergrowth?

Yes! The man had his back to Chip, and was bent down close to the ground, fiddling at something in his hands. Chip stayed as still and as quiet as he possibly could. His heart was pounding in his ears and he could only pray it wasn't as loud in reality as it was in his imagination.

He looked to the other side of the corrals, nearer to the campsite itself, and tried to judge the activity going on there. He could see that many of the fire crews had already moved out. Those that were left were busy stowing their gear and cleaning up the area.

He did not spot the person he assumed to be his assailant among them. Most likely it was the man closer to the stables.

Quickly, he turned about, and retraced his steps back to the main trail. As he walked, he zipped up his still-damp windbreaker and pulled the collar up around his neck. He reached down in his pocket and pulled out a woolen watch cap. It was wet, but he crammed it down over his head and ears anyway.

As he entered into the compound, he skirted the area closest to the corrals and walked rapidly down the other side of the open area. Those left were busy with their own affairs and hardly glanced up at him as he passed.

Praying that no one would recognize him or try to stop him, he nearly made the outer road when a voice rang out.

"Hey, you!—Yes, I mean you! Hold up there a minute. I want to talk to you."

Chip froze and slowly turned around, expecting the worst.

The man doing the talking was on the far side of the compound—and he was looking in the opposite direction at one of the other crew members.

Chip turned back and continued walking as fast as he could without looking as if he was trying to run away. This time, instead of skirting the site, he headed straight down the middle toward the exit to the outer road where he had parked his car.

Now if only his car was still there and no one had tampered with it.

There it was! He spotted it immediately, at the far end of the dirt track near the turn off onto the macadam road leading back to Cedar Pines Park. Leaving caution to the winds, he broke into a jog. Every bone and muscle in his body protested, but he paid the discomfort no mind.

He reached the car and gave it a quick onceover from the outside. It looked to be exactly as he had left it. Now, if he could only get in and start it up.

He had not thought about the key fob. Was it still in his pants after his dip in the cavern pond? And if so, was it still functioning?

He jammed his fist down deep into the front change pocket and scrabbled around with his fingers. He nearly panicked at first, thinking he had lost it. But, no, there it was!

He grabbed the fob and hauled it out of his sodden pants and, hands trembling, pointed it at the car and pushed the button. Nothing happened at first. But the second time he jabbed, aiming more directly, there was a faint squeak as the car lock popped open.

Chip grabbed the handle and pulled, a little harder than necessary, opened up the driver's side door and fell into the front seat. He reached over, grabbed the door and slammed it, setting the lock again as he did so.

For a moment he just sat there, breathing hard in relief. Then, heart in mouth, he took the key in his trembling hand, pushed it into the ignition slot, and turned it.

Nothing happened. Was it possible that the assailant had scuttled the car, removed the battery, for instance—or cut the cables?

Carefully, he took a firmer hold of the key and tried again. This time there was a brief sputter. He pumped the gas pedal a time or two before trying the third time.

Vroom! The response was sudden and startled him so that he nearly let the motor die again. But he rallied, eased the gas pedal up and down slightly, judging the engine's response.

Soon the car was purring like a cat. He glanced hopefully at the gas gauge. He still had half a tank of gas. That should be enough to get him in to the Cedar Pines Park area, or even as far as Lake Silverwood, where he had passed several stations on the way in to Camp Seely.

He looked up and down the road and saw no moving vehicles near him. Cautiously, he put the car in gear, got it turned around, and headed back up the road toward the main highway.

Once there he would watch for a service station and while getting the car filled, he could make a pay phone call to Everett Hightower. He only hoped nothing else would happen to prevent him.

* * * *

In the greater scheme of things, it might not have made any difference to the outcome at all. But given the role coincidence had played in their little adventure, Richard couldn't help but feel that he had somehow lost complete control of the present situation.

And he now felt responsible for the lives of his friends.

He could only sit and wait and hope for information of any kind to come trickling in. There seemed to be no way he and Everett Hightower could intervene, and it irked him no end that he had allowed things to get so out of hand.

Most troubling of all was the lack of contact from Chip, and now Dave was late in checking in. Carl was miles away in another trouble zone. The morning after their conversation, Sacramento had contacted him about the possibility of a flare up at the Yuba River site.

"Have you talked to Carl Frick out there yet?" he said.

"No," the man said. "As a matter of fact, that's one of the things I wanted to talk to *you* about. I haven't been able to get in touch with him this morning. He seems to have shut his phone off or something. I was going to let him know about this new flare up, seeing as how he's right in that location."

"You say you can't get hold of him?" Richard was beginning to panic now. Were all three of them now out of contact?

"No. I thought maybe you had already suggested he come back here."

"I spoke to him last night and the only thing he said was he had gotten hold of some map out to the origin of the first fire. We talked about him coming back but then it was decided he would stay out there another day or see and see what he could turn up."

"Well, all I can do is request that the crews keep an eye out for him. I guess no one knows he's investigating the fires?"

"We thought it would be best if he stayed undercover for the time being," Richard said. "Do you think it's wise to change that strategy now?"

"Look, it's really your call, I guess," the man said. "But if it were me, I'd want to get him out of there any way possible. You have no idea how treacherous these flare ups can be. We've had whole crews wiped out in a few minutes just because they got trapped and couldn't get out of the way of the fire in time."

"All right," Richard said. "Go ahead and get the word out to the crews on the line to be on the lookout for him. I guess that's the only option we have now."

TEN

David Spaulding awoke with a start to the alarm which he had set for 8:00 a.m. He was stiff and cranky, his mouth was dry, and his muscles were sore.

He rose, though, showered, shaved, and dressed, and set about to face the day before him.

When he opened the blinds he was greeted with bright sunshine and a clear blue sky. He hoped they were good omens for a profitable search, but he scarcely dared rely on it. He knew better than to put his trust in something as unreliable as luck.

He checked that he had his wallet on him and his phone safely buttoned away, grabbed the leather attaché case which rarely left his side, and headed out and down the hall to the elevators.

A few other sleepy souls were gathered there waiting for the "Down" car. He squeezed in with the rest of the group, pushed the button for the "2nd Floor," and prepared for whatever mood Carmen had chosen for this day.

He knocked on her door three times, a prearranged signal they had been using, and was more than surprised when she opened it immediately. She must have been standing right there waiting for his arrival, he reasoned.

Or perhaps she was merely anticipating the breakfast service she had promised to order.

In any case, he greeted her with as much cheerfulness and good humor as he could muster, given his restless night, and she stepped back to let him enter.

She was dressed conservatively as usual, in a subdued navy pant suit, an attractive coordinating blouse, and sensible walking shoes. Her hair was shiny, as if she had just shampooed it—and once again, he detected a subtle trace of the scent which had overwhelmed him in the library the day before.

"Come on in, Dave," she said, gesturing toward a table in the living area. "You're right on schedule. They just delivered our breakfast cart a few minutes ago.

"I hope you're hungry," she added with a smile. "I might have gone a little overboard when I ordered."

"Good morning, Carmen," he said, with what he hoped sounded like a cheerful greeting.

"I hope you're feeling a lot better today," he added, setting his attaché case down next to the couch. "I was quite worried about you last night."

"Oh thanks," she said, with a toss of her head. "But I'm all right. I tend to get these headaches whenever I'm a little stressed out. I don't think they're as bad as migraines, but it's still a nuisance."

"I can imagine," he said. "Have you ever seen a doctor about it?"

He wished he could take back the question the moment it was out of his mouth. He had been so determined not to get too personal with her today, and here he was asking her about her health care.

She hesitated a moment before answering.

"No, Dave, I haven't. My health seems fine otherwise, and the headaches never seem to last all that long. Also, I don't want to get started taking a bunch of pills.

"Now," she said, changing the subject, "Let's go over to the table and have our breakfast. May I pour you some coffee? And then I think we can just help ourselves, if you like."

They took their seats in comfortable upholstered chairs at the table and after pouring out their coffee, Carmen began handing around the steaming platters.

In spite of the terrible night he'd had, Dave began relaxing in spite of himself. He sat back at his ease in the pleasant sunlit room and began taking an interest in the various dishes put before him.

"This all tastes great," he said, between bites of omelet and sausage. "Thanks again, Carmen," he added, "...for setting this up for us. It was a good idea."

"I'm so glad you're enjoying it," she murmured, sitting back with her coffee. She had taken much smaller helpings than Dave, mostly of fruit and toast. "I thought a nourishing meal would get us off to a good start today."

"Yes," he said. "I wanted to talk to you about that. I think maybe I was a little pushy yesterday. The problem is, when I get on the scent of a story, I can be pretty obsessive. I think I owe you an apology. This is definitely your investigation, and I should be keeping my big mouth shut and letting you call the shots.

"It's just my bullish nature, I guess," he added with a grin.

She eyed him over her cup.

"Well," she said. "I suspect that admission is a first for you."

She laughed then and went on. "Take it easy Dave. Just as I said yesterday, I had a splitting headache and I was really tired. To be perfectly honest, I think you did a masterful job planning our research. And we got results—good ones. I think Hightower is going to be very surprised at all the information we've put together. And it's only been a couple of days after all.

"No," she concluded. "You meant no offense, I'm sure—and none was taken on my end. Let's finish our meal and plan out our next move. I have a feeling there will be even more surprises in store for us today."

Dave wanted to feel relief at Carmen's conciliatory words. But instead he began to feel an eerie prickly sensation at the back of his neck.

He shook his head and tried in vain to remember everything Richard had been saying to him about who Carmen might really be—and in particular his friend's warnings about getting overly involved with her.

Strangely, it now all seemed like a jumble in his mind.

Still, there she was, beckoning to him, and urging him to get up out of his seat and get ready for their searches for the day.

"Here," she said, helping him to his feet. "I intend to take the Land Rover today. You've been doing all the driving and it's my turn now. Besides, I already have some pretty good ideas about where we should start.

"Come on, now, Dave," she added. "Don't worry about the food and all that. The help will take care of it once we leave."

So saying, she grabbed him by the arm and led him, stumbling a bit, out and down the hall to the elevators. Once on the ground level, she steered him not into the lobby but out a side door which led straight in to the parking lot. There she opened the door to the passenger seat of the Land Rover waiting nearby.

"Here," she said, as she helped him in and buckled his seat belt for him tightly. "If you like, I can let the seat down a bit so you can lie back and relax. And here's a nice pillow I brought for you." She fluffed it up and placed it behind his head.

"Take a little nap if you like," she added. "We'll be on the road for a few hours."

David Spaulding although silent through her ministering, was acutely aware, somewhere in the extreme back of his brain, that something in his world had gone terribly wrong over the past hour. He seemed powerless to resist any of Carmen's suggestions—and he could think of no good reason why he should.

As they headed off into the morning sun, he heard something that sounded like the drumming of wings in his ears. He had the bizarre sensation that he had become some sort of captured bird who had lost the will to live.

* * * *

Carmen entered the freeway off of Hospitality Row and headed north via I-215 toward the Cajon Pass. It was just a little past 9:00 a.m. They were right on time and—with any luck—she would reach her final goal by mid to late afternoon.

She had checked the Land Rover's specs and its gas tank capacity should allow her to cover about 600 miles on one fill up—which should be more than adequate for her purposes. It would be better if she didn't have to stop for fuel with him here in the car with her, even at some remote station. Of course she could always throw a blanket over him if necessary.

She smiled at the idea and glanced over at Dave, lying back and securely strapped into the passenger seat. His head was lolling to one side, a drop of spittle at the corner of his mouth, and his wide open eyes were glazed over in an uncomprehending stare.

Good! The dose of sedative she had placed in his morning coffee had been exactly the right amount, just as she had estimated. He should remain in this coma-like state for at least a couple of hours. That would be long enough for her to get a little further north into a more deserted part of the desert before she stopped off the road to take care of the next phase of her plan.

She hummed a cheery French ditty from her Canadian days as she drove. It was a beautiful morning and she felt light and free as a bird. Soon she would no longer need to look over her shoulder and second guess each and every thing she said or did.

David Spaulding might be a crack detective. But she, a mere woman, had completely outsmarted him. She was in control of the situation now. And she intended to remain that way.

Once they passed through the desert town of Adelanto the businesses began to thin out more and more. Soon there would be nothing but bleak landscape until they reached Kramer Junction, a major crossroads before turning off toward their final destination. She would make the decision there whether or not she should refuel.

She began watching along the side of the mostly deserted highway until she finally spotted a turnout onto a side road with what looked like a deserted shack at the end. She pulled onto it and bounced down the uneven dirt track to the falling down structure and stopped.

After getting out and looking around, she decided all was clear and returned to the passenger side of the car. This would be the tricky part.

Carefully she undid the seat belt and rolled Dave over on his side toward the driver's seat. With practiced skill she maneuvered his hands around and behind his back and tightly bound them together with sturdy cords she had stored in the console. She tested the knots several times and once she was certain they were secure, she rolled Dave back over on to the seat.

She straightened him out as best she could and buckled him back in again, pulling the strap as tight as possible. Then she pulled his feet together and bound them too.

Carmen inspected her handiwork and chuckled. Dave was going to be sore and uncomfortable when he came to, but she still knew all the tricks of her craft.

This little birdie was all trussed up and going nowhere.

She got behind the wheel again, reexamined her GPS to make sure she was on the correct route, checked the Land Rover's gas level, and headed back out to the main highway.

She continued driving at a steady pace making sure to keep to the posted speed limit and following all of the rules of the road. The last thing she needed now was to be stopped by some State Trooper fulfilling his ticket quota. She could probably make some sort of explanation that David was merely dozing after his turn at the wheel. But there was no certainty that an over-zealous cop might not decide to check the veracity of her claim.

And such a request would necessitate other actions she did not want to be forced to take right now. No. It was far better to go at a reasonable speed, even out in this god-forsaken desert and hope she would make it through unnoticed and unchallenged.

Just as she had predicted, Dave began showing signs of coming out of his stupor about three hours into the trip.

"Ow," he said, struggling against his bonds. "What did you do to me?"

"Good morning," she said cheerfully. "Welcome back to the land of the living. Don't worry," she added. "You'll survive—for now."

He blinked his eyes at the sun streaming on to his face. The fact that he had been staring straight into the light with unseeing eyes had resulted in semi-blindness, temporary, he hoped.

His mouth was dry and there was a strange, bitter aftertaste at the back of his throat. He coughed and tried to sit up a little straighter.

That was when he realized he was bound hand and foot. Together with the seat belt strapped tightly around him, he couldn't move. His arms ached and he began to panic.

"Come on, Carmen," he said. "What the hell do you think you're trying to pull here? Whatever your problem is, I promise you it has nothing to do with me.

"Stop the car," he added. "Let's talk this out."

:"Not a chance," she said. "You and I both know what this is all about. I have no choice in the matter. Now, I advise you to just sit back and enjoy the ride. We have quite a ways yet to go before we reach our destination. You're going to need all the strength you can muster then, Spaulding. So my advice to you is to shut up and get some rest.

"And if you don't keep quiet," she cautioned, "I can always put a gag on you. Trust me. That will make things even worse for you."

So he kept quiet.

But his mind was working. Now that the sedative had worn off, he realized that he was going to have to figure out some way of outsmarting the she devil (for that was how he thought of her now) or making a convincing argument to her to stop this foolishness and release him.

The trouble was, he still had no idea what her real name was and what connection he had with her before. One thing was certain now. Her name was *not* Carmen Ruiz.

He knew he had few if any, acceptable alternatives to what she had in mind for him. Would money do it? Could he bribe her to just walk away from this nonsense with his promise of no further interference from him?

He began to plot just how he would make such a proposition. He knew that the further they got out into the desert, the fewer his opportunities for escape might be.

Dave's one hope was that Richard might be able to track down their progress and call for government assistance at some point. He had given his friend the make, model, and license number of the Land Rover on the first day. The authorities might be able to track their progress via satellite.

Surreptitiously, he thought, he tested his bonds, moving his arms back and forth a little as if to get into a more comfortable position.

"Stop it," she said almost instantly. "That wiggling around isn't going to do you one bit of good. The more you try to pull on the cords, the tighter they will get. You'll only make things a whole lot more uncomfortable for yourself."

"My arms are going to sleep," he said. "Can't you at least help me raise them up a bit? The pain really is getting unbearable."

Maybe, he hoped, he could plead to her humanity.

"So what?" she laughed. "Why in the world do you think I care anything about your so-called comfort now?"

"But *why* are you doing this to me? I've done nothing to you—at least not to my knowledge." He was appealing to her reason.

"I can make all kinds of amends to you," he went on. "—money—a fresh start somewhere else. I'm willing to help you do anything you want or need—in complete confidence if necessary. Just say the word."

There. He had made an offer of sorts. It was entirely up to her now. Perhaps she would counteroffer with some other request. He knew he was desperate enough to comply with any demands she might make, reasonable or not.

All he wanted in return was his freedom.

There was a brief silence as she appeared to be thinking over the new options he had presented.

"It's really not as easy as all that, you know," Carmen said finally. "I'm afraid none of what you suggest is possible. It's too late for anything like that."

She consulted her GPS again and turned off the main highway on to a bumpy side road heading off toward the east, as nearly as he could judge.

His heart was pounding with fear and panic. What on earth was she planning to do with him out here in this deserted wilderness? One thing was certain. Whatever his fate, there would be no witnesses to her crime.

ELEVEN

"Why don't you just kill me, Carmen, and be done with it?"

She ignored his question, which was a stupid one, if he would only think about it.

As he well knew, there were too many public connections between them at this point. She couldn't be sure of how much back up support he had—and how close on the trail they might be. And finally, she still wasn't at all sure how much he knew—or had guessed—about her true identity.

With any luck at all, he was still completely in the dark on that last point, but it wasn't a certainty.

In the case of her Caribbean rescuer, Larry, on the other hand, there had been no previous connection at all between the two of them and they had never been seen together. More importantly, there had been a very effective way of disposing of his body. And there was at least a chance Larry's demise would go undiscovered for a very long time—perhaps even forever.

Not so in the case of David Spaulding. In whatever governmental capacity he was working at the moment, people would be looking for him and tracking his every movement. As Carmen Ruiz, she had been seen with him in public on multiple occasions and their working relationship had been well established through their meetings with Everett Hightower, an unimpeachable source.

And if she *had* given Dave enough poison to kill him in advance of dumping his body out here on the desert, that act alone would go a long way toward establishing concrete evidence of her guilt of premeditated murder. At least this way she had a fighting chance of pleading non-culpability in his demise.

It was worth a shot anyway.

David said nothing more, but he thought he already knew at least part of the answer to his questions. Carmen, if that was her real name—and he was certain now that it wasn't—was no better than the arsonist they had been trying to track down for the past few days. The fire-starter was nothing more than a monster that enjoyed watching tiny living creatures fry to a crisp within a prism of colored glass.

And Carmen, it seemed, was seeking self-redemption in the torture of others.

She continued to push the Land Rover forward across the steaming salt flats, heading slightly north now into the fading light.

Finally she stopped and stepped out into the blast furnace which was Death Valley in the daytime and looked around.

"Come on," she said, almost gleefully, unbuckling the seat belt, grabbing him by the shoulder, and pulling him out onto the hardened sand. "It's time for your close-up, Mr. Spaulding!"

Dave was still dizzy. He stumbled, trying to right himself in spite of the cords wrapped around his feet and binding his arms at the back.

"Well, won't you at least untie my feet—so I can walk? Give me half a chance, won't you?"

She laughed out loud, and the tinkling sound echoed away across the panhandle, and reverberated sharply against the mountains barely visible in the distance.

"Now, why in God's name would I do that?" she said. "Are you stupid? I'd rather imagine you as you are right now you pig—hog-tied and helpless. What is it they say about your kind—the '*Mounties always get their man*'? All I'm concerned about here is buying a little more time for myself—as much of it as possible in fact. It's not likely you can convince me to make it that much easier for you to escape your fate."

She turned business-like then, spinning him around and pointing off into the distance.

"See that?" she said, gesturing to the southeast. "That very pale light you see way off there in the sky in the distance is the grand old city of Las Vegas. All you have to do is head toward that light and you will find salvation.

"And there is a highway of sorts, further to the south out there somewhere. If you can reach that, you might be lucky enough to run across a motorist crossing this God-forsaken desert. And if they're not scared to death at the sight of you, they might even stop and give you a lift."

He squinted at the horizon in the direction she had indicated. If what she was saying was true, and there was no reason to believe otherwise, he reckoned it had to be about 80 miles, more or less, to get anywhere near that soft glow indicating city lights.

But if there *was* a highway out there, too—well, that might be an even better possibility.

"Is there any chance I can talk you into leaving me some water?" he asked, hoping against hope that she would be a little relenting.

"Hah! Not on your *bloody* life!"

She blinked and paused, just for a moment, wrinkling her brow—as if she hadn't meant to say exactly that. Then she laughed out loud again at the little joke she had made.

"You are definitely on your own now, Spaulding," she continued. "Let's just see what good all of your fancy police training will do for you now!"

And with that final thought, she shoved him down on the ground, hard, strode back to the waiting Land Rover, and drove off into the growing dusk.

As the vehicle disappeared into the distance, David Spaulding lay very still there on the floor of Death Valley for a few moments, trying to calm his beating heart and throw off the panic that threatened to overwhelm him.

Then, slowly and carefully, he maneuvered into a sitting position and took stock of his situation. After thinking it through, he rallied, and with what felt like a superhuman effort, the kind you would use if you were trying to move a car off a child, he pulled his tied arms down, scrunching them under his butt, paused a moment to catch his breath, then continued manipulating his hands up and over his bound feet.

His shoulders hurt like hell when he was done, but at the end of it at least his hands were in front of him, as they ought to be, and of better use to him.

He heaved a tremendous sigh of relief and thankfulness for all the survival training he had been given recently and began at once working away with his fingers, as best he could, at the knots binding his feet.

If he could at least stand and walk upright, he might have a chance—of a snowball freezing in Hell, he thought, laughing inwardly at the insanity of it all.

First he carefully tried to analyze the knots she'd used. Then he began, bit by bit, to worry away at what looked to be the loose ends, cheering inwardly when he could feel a bit of give and slippage, and crying out loud in anger and frustration when he couldn't move an obstacle.

The dying sun had nearly sunk below the horizon into the west by the time he triumphantly slipped the last of the cords off his feet. He considered whether he should take the time while still seated there to work on his hands, flapping as they were somewhat uselessly in front of him.

Or should he struggle to his feet and just start walking? Sweat was pouring off him, in spite of the gradually darkening sky.

The worst of it was the knowledge that he had no water—and very little prayer of finding any out here.

He knew one thing for certain. Doing nothing was not an option.

The main highway, as she had described it, appeared to run from west to east through the small town of Pahrump, as near as he could remember, and ended up in Las Vegas, Nevada. It looked to him, as he squinted off at the glow in the distance, to be about 80 miles, more or less, from where she had dropped him—just as he had guessed earlier.

Eighty miles he reckoned—*and if I try to walk that distance without water I'll surely be dead before I get there*, he thought frantically.

If he could reach that highway running parallel, though, and if—*big if*—he could flag down any random vehicle coming down that deserted road in the middle of the night and at the exact right moment, he might be able to save himself. Pahrump, he decided, was useless. It was a small town and, without Vegas's glow to light his way, he couldn't be at all sure of hitting it exactly on foot.

Of course none of any of it was a sure thing at all.

And David Spaulding did not like to rely on outcomes that were not certain.

He turned around then and stared off westward into the distance behind him. There he saw foothills, rocky cliffs, and mountains that seemed to his naked eye, to be somewhat closer in range than Las Vegas.

There was no absolute certainty of water or shelter in that direction, either. Still, he thought, the possibilities in the higher elevations were a hell of a lot better than a long hike through the blazing desert to Las Vegas—or even the highway.

Suddenly he straightened up and took another hard look. If he squinted just a bit he could barely make out, in the rapidly deepening twilight, a smaller, darker shape roughly outlined against the much larger rock facing behind.

If that shape indicated a small hillock or stand of brush of *any* kind, it might provide a bit of shade or shelter against the blazing sun that he knew he would be facing at dawn. It might even be a deserted miner's cabin. It was difficult to judge the distance from where he stood, but it looked a hell of a lot closer than Las Vegas in the roughly opposite direction.

If he could find any small bit of cover there, it might be his salvation.

Water, of course, was another thing altogether. How long could a human being last without it? Three or four days, he thought. He tried to remember all of his survival techniques and training. There were some plants, cacti, for example, which might provide a wee bit of moisture if chewed. Or he could dig down into the sand and, hopefully, strike a deposit of liquid left over from some previous precipitation.

There were no certain answers to all these questions. But just standing here thinking about it would gain him nothing.

With very little hope of surviving the trek ahead of him, he struck out in the direction of the shadowy object in front of the cliffs, working at the ties binding his hands with his teeth as he walked. He was headed, roughly, "north by northwest," he thought, laughing out loud this time at the insanity of his situation.

All he could think about was the last meal he had consumed—and the tall glass of ice water he had downed so casually afterwards.

He thought that he would gladly give his soul right then and there, to be back at that last supper.

* * * *

The terrain he was going to be crossing looked to be some sort of large salt flat which could make his journey somewhat easier. It was eerily silent. He turned toward the outcropping of rock, spotted the darkened area again, and set out in that direction.

And then the first of several miracles occurred.

He was overjoyed when he began to realize, as night overtook the land, that he had been blessed with a full moon. Gradually, the bright orb climbed up into the sky, casting a subdued glow over the landscape.

At least, with some light from above to show the way, he had much less risk of tripping or falling. He was mostly afraid of injuring or incapacitating himself in some manner, either by stepping into a pothole, or blundering into a stone or bush of some sort. There didn't appear to be anything like that out here on the flats but, as he had learned so often in the past, there was always the exception to every rule.

He tried to stick to a regular pace, but it was difficult, to maintain it and still keep an eagle eye out for hazards. He walked slowly and steadily, but his heart was beating with apprehension. He could not see how he could keep up a steady speed if, all the while, he was anticipating a disastrous accident.

Finally he stopped to take stock again. It did not appear to him that he had made much of any progress at all toward the dark spot that was his goal, although that was probably an illusion. He just hoped the vision in front of him was not some kind of mirage.

Still, he hoped that getting to higher ground would work to his advantage. There might be some sort of shade, shelter, and even water, at those elevations. He would just have to follow the plan—and not give up prematurely.

Then the second miracle took place. As Dave shuffled along, his toe hit something hard, both startling him and causing him to stumble at the same time. He managed to catch himself before falling and looked down at his feet to see what had tripped him up.

It was a stick or pole of some kind. He reached down and gingerly picked it up, examining it carefully as best he could in the moonlight.

He realized at once that it had been some sort of fence post or something similar. It was a solid piece of wood, about 2" or 3" in diameter, and looked to be approximately 5' in length. He had no idea what it was doing out here in the middle of the salt flats, but here it was—and it was exactly the right size and length to serve as a walking stick.

Quickly, he pulled out one of the cords he had saved from his foot bindings and managed, using his teeth and available fingers to wrap it round and round one tip of the post, tucking the end in as securely as possible—and thus creating a kind of handhold.

The new walking stick was a godsend, as it turned out. He soon realized that to keep to the direction leading to the stain on the cliffs, he would have to leave the flats onto more uneven ground. His improvised cane would help prevent future stumbles and having it to rely upon gave him the confidence to keep up his speed in the rougher terrain.

Thanking his lucky stars—and there were many of them out there in that endless night sky—David Spaulding continued on his journey into the unknown. His hands were still bound, but he had been working away at the cords with his teeth and free fingers.

Something was bound to come loose soon.

And then, he vowed, nothing would stop him from his goal.

He soon developed a strategy of sorts, using the stick as a kind of pole vault, thrusting it forward ahead of him, hitting pay dirt and sticking it, then jogging up to it. There he would pause for a moment to catch his breath and work a bit at one of the knots binding his hands.

It was slow going, but at least he felt like he was making some sort of slow progress. He was beginning to despair of actually reaching the dark stain on the cliffs before daylight, but the closer he got to it the better off he would be, he thought.

And then about thirty minutes into the journey with this process, the next miracle took place.

On one of his frequent rest sessions, while he was worrying away at the hand bindings, he felt the knot slip a bit. He worked furiously then, pulling and gnawing at the loose bit of cord—until the whole thing came apart in his mouth.

He spit it out and began edging his hands and fingers, back and forth, up and down, searching for yet another loose tie. And, as luck would have it, the killer knot had been the key. Once the cord had slipped out of its stranglehold, the rest of the structure came slipping away, too.

Shaking his hands furiously to get the blood flowing again, he felt, rather than saw, the last of the bonds restricting his movement fall away to the ground.

He stood still there for a moment, relishing this sweet victory.

Now that he was unfettered, with the walking stick to ease his way, and a plausible goal before him, he had a fighting chance. And best of all, there was the beautiful moon to light his way.

He continued his technique of using the stick as a pole vaulter would, thrusting it out in front of him, jogging a few steps up to it—thrust jog thrust—before stopping a moment or two to catch his breath. It felt as if he was making progress.

Every so often he would scan the horizon just to be sure he was still on track. The bright moonlight still etched the outline of the dark blotch against the outcropping of rock. And as he moved closer to it he became even more heartened that it represented, if nothing else, an anomaly—a difference in the landscape which might represent some sort of useful substitute for shelter.

And, as he moved forward, his mind kept whirling around the disturbing events of the past few hours—mainly about how he had gotten himself into this predicament.

The key, of course, was the woman, Carmen.

Who was she, really? She had presented herself to him as an attractive woman and a competent investigator—much like himself—who was using every tool at her command to find the mystery arsonist and bring him (or her) to justice.

He had been stupid, he realized, to allow himself to be manipulated by her. Yes. She *was* an attractive woman. But he should have been more circumspect. He had taken to heart Richard Black Wolf's advice about getting out and in the game again. But just because he had felt a fluttering of interest—desire even—he should not have become involved so quickly with someone about whom he knew so little.

And what *did* he know about her?

There was a little ping, in the back of his brain, that told him he was missing something important. And he had learned, over time, to pay close attention to that ping. First of all, there was something about her that seemed—what was it?—*familiar*. Yes. That was it. It was almost as if he recognized her from some previous situation. And secondly, there was also something about her speech patterns that did not ring true. And if she wasn't of Cuban heritage, born and bred in Miami—then where *was* she from?—and why was she so vindictive toward him?

Yet, for the life of him, he could not put his finger on it.

All of a sudden he tripped, caught himself with the stick, and came up short. He had stepped into a pothole and had nearly taken a tumble. He took stock. His foot and ankle seemed all right. But he would definitely need to stay more alert. He could not afford to fall and perhaps break a bone or sprain his ankle. He would really be a goner if that happened.

He stopped and rested a bit, still straining his eyes toward his far off goal. He could see what had happened. In order to maintain his direction toward the outcropping, he was gradually leaving the flat salt bed and moving on to rougher terrain. Now there were a few scraggly growths of vegetation here and there. The smooth packed sand had turned to an uneven gravelly texture, including potholes and larger rocks scattered about.

He looked up again at the blotch. It seemed much larger now. He still could not discern exactly what it was. But there definitely was *something* there.

He judged now that he was not more than a dozen miles away from the cliff at the most. The moon was still shining brightly across his path.

But there was also a new glow just above the horizon to the east.

Here comes the sun he thought. I need to pick up the pace if I'm actually going to pull this off.

* * * *

He changed his method to straight jogging, plunking the stick down beside him as he ran. He could only manage a minute or two before stopping to catch his breath, but he did seem to be making better progress.

He kept his eye on the prize and was greatly encouraged as it appeared to draw nearer. It didn't seem quite so massive now, as it had appeared from a distance. He wondered, not for the first time, if this wasn't just some giant act of desperation which would end in defeat.

But he was committed now. At least the rock outcropping, together with his lucky stick, might enable him to create some sort of shade structure with his clothing. Even such minimum shelter from the sun might be just enough to keep him alive until nightfall. And the higher elevation might provide some bit of breeze.

He was several more hours into it, and the pink fingers of dawn were beginning to displace the moon, when he actually could begin to make out details on the rock outcropping itself, looming up, practically in front of him now.

He stopped again to catch his breath and massage his aching muscles—and groaned in disappointment.

Just as he had feared, the dark mass outlined against the rock face was nothing more than a framework of some sort. It appeared to be made of several railroad ties strung together with old two by fours. All of the wood was darkened by age and, perhaps, some kind of preservative oils.

But what was its purpose? What could it possibly be?

He slowed down now. No point in killing himself. He was nearly there. He tried to imagine a purpose for a wooden framework backed up to a rock outcropping and stuck way out here in the middle of nowhere. He could think of none that made any sense.

Finally he broke into a cleared area in front of the edifice, whatever it was, and stopped altogether.

Just then he heard something which, in his mind, sounded very much like another small miracle headed his way.

Was that a clap of thunder? Could it be possible? Was he about to be the recipient of one of those extremely rare summer cloudbursts, way out here in the middle of the hell known as Death Valley?

But if there was any brief downpour coming his way, how in the world would he be able to capture any of the precious liquid which might possibly mean the difference between life and death for him?

He thought frantically then started looking around on the desert floor for something—*anything*—which might serve as a container of sorts.

And then he spotted it, half buried in the sand just off to one side of the wooden frame. It was an old tin can, stripped of any paper label, but it looked to be about the size of a #10 can of something like tomatoes or beans.

He ran to it and pried it up out of its bed. It was heavy, and it took a minute to free it. He saw there was something down inside and quickly turned it over and emptied it out—dirt, a few rocks, and there, glinting in the first rays of sunlight drifting across the clearing, lay a bright shiny key.

His first act was to place the emptied tin can back in the hollowed out spot steadied by a few of the rocks. There. That would capture any possible rain drops that might come in this direction.

Next he picked up the key and examined it carefully. It was a standard deadbolt key, and it seemed to be of fairly new vintage.

Dave looked back at the dark wooden framework. A light went off in his brain.

He ran, loping crazily, to the middle of the frame and examined it more carefully this time.

No. This truly was the *real* miracle. With bated breath and shaking hands, he placed the key into a barely discernible lock within the darkened frame which he had failed to notice at first glance.

It turned smoothly, with no problem. There was a faint click and tugging at the frame gently, he swung open the door—for that, indeed, was what it was— and peered hopefully inside.

At first, he could see nothing. It seemed to be completely dark within, and his heart sank a bit. It would be difficult to make use of the space inside without some sort of light. But when he stepped gingerly across the threshold there was a sudden loud whooshing noise and an overhead light burst on, nearly blinding him at first. At the same time, a large ceiling fan began spinning, round and round, whirring gently, and stirring the slightly muggy air.

He carefully slipped the key into his shirt pocket, buttoned it down, and patted it several times, just to make sure it was safely secured.

Then he stepped back outside into the clearing and glanced up over the top of the framework, noticing for the very first time two small solar panels, now greedily gobbling up the dawn's early light.

Why had he not noticed those panels before? Never mind. They were there all right, cleverly camouflaged by the ancient wood framing.

David Spaulding was nearly sobbing out loud now, and tears of joy and relief streamed down his stubbly cheeks.

Safe! He was safe and saved! All that he had endured before no longer mattered now—the hours of struggle—the fear and exhaustion. Nothing else mattered now, but that he had found usable, workable shelter—and he was safe.

He reentered the room (for such it was) carved back in and under the rocky outcrop and, after a moment of hesitation, he retrieved the key again, pulled the door closed behind him, and relocked the deadbolt securely from the inside.

He had no idea who had set up this haven. But discretion being the better part of valor, he preferred to have some warning before that unknown party might return and confront him trespassing here.

He took his time then and looked about with great curiosity. The light was bright enough to shine into all the dark corners, and the white noise of the whirring fan was both refreshing and comforting.

He took a deep breath and began to explore his surroundings.

A sturdy square wooden table and two matching chairs sat directly under the light. A wooden counter along one side of the room held a small microwave, a mini-refrigerator, and a box full of provisions, including bottled water, energy bars, and individual cans of things like pork-and-beans, stew, and soup.

Out of curiosity, he opened the tiny frig and discovered a six-pack of water and one of energy drinks. The little motor was churning away now, and the inside walls were already cooling down nicely.

On the opposite side of the room, behind a draped curtain, sat a chemical toilet flanked by a tiny night stand holding an enamel basin. Nearby was a pitcher full of water. He would not drink that water, he decided, since it might not be potable. But at least he would be able to rinse some of the sweat and grime off his hands and face.

A comfy-looking built-in bed stretched across the back of the cavern room. It was piled with pillows and a comforter, just waiting for a weary traveler to sample its wares.

But first things came first. He took advantage of the lavatory, washed up, and then eyed his food choices. He decided not to overdo, not knowing how long he would need to rely on the cavern's offerings. He selected just a bottle of water and one of the energy bars, carried them over to the tiny table, and sat down to eat.

He glanced down at a notepad lying there, wondering if the owner had left any clue as to his identity. But it appeared to be blank. He chewed quickly, washing the dry bar down with the water.

Thankful, thankful, thankful, were the only thoughts he could muster at the moment. He was thankful he had survived his ordeal thus far, and equally thankful he had made a good decision about this place.

A few minutes later, rumbling stomach satisfied and thirst slaked, he made his way over to the bed. There was a small lamp on the built-in shelf next to it and he switched it on. The light was sufficient to allow him to make his way around, but dim enough for sleeping. He glanced back. Sure enough there was a pull chain on the brighter overhead light and he switched it off.

His phantom host had thought of everything.

Slipping off his dusty shoes, he climbed beneath the comforter and rested his head on a fluffy pillow. The linens seemed fresh and the bed was beyond comfortable to his aching body.

In a few minutes, David Spaulding's gentle snores were keeping pace with the overhead swoosh of the fan.

It had been a very long night.

TWELVE

At first he thought he probably wouldn't be able to sleep, in spite of his relief at finding sanctuary in (what was it?) the miner's cabin. So much had happened over the past twenty-four hours that his mind seemed to be spinning wildly out of control.

Not to mention the mere fact that he was bone tired and aching from head to toe after his horrendous hike across the salt flats.

But his exhaustion took precedence—evidently—because no sooner had his head hit the pillow then he fell into a dreamless healing sleep—almost like a coma—from which he didn't wake for some hours.

When he did open his eyes finally, it took him a moment or two to regain his bearings and remember where he was—and all the circumstances that had led him here.

The cooling fan was still whirring away overhead. But now the overhead light was on, blazing down into his sleep-startled eyes.

He sat up immediately and stared into the face of a stranger—a man dressed all in black—standing, arms akimbo, and glaring at him from across the room.

"Who the hell are you?" the newcomer growled. "And how did you manage to break in here/"

Dave struggled to gather his thoughts, shaking his head, and trying to figure out the best way to approach this confrontation.

He gently eased his hands out from under the comforter and laid them in front of his chest, palms up, so the man could see he wasn't armed. Then slowly, very slowly, with no sudden moves, he inched his way into a sitting position and allowed the covers to fall away from him.

Nothing to see here, he wanted the stranger to believe. There is nothing threatening to see here at all.

He cleared his throat. "My name is David Spaulding," he said. "I got stranded without water out there on the salt flats last night. I spotted this rock outcropping and decided to make my way toward it in hopes of finding some shade and even some water, before the sun came up."

The man nodded. "Go on."

"It took me hours of walking. A couple of times I nearly gave up hope and I thought I was probably going to die out there. But I kept going—heading for this spot. I finally got to the clearing out front just as the sun was starting to come up."

"But just how did you get inside?" the man said. He was insistent on that point. Dave could tell it really concerned him that someone had managed to break in to his private place without actually tearing the door down.

"Well," Dave said. "As I was standing outside there, trying to figure out what this place was—at the time I didn't realize there was a room behind the framework out there—just while I was standing there I heard what sounded to me like thunder. All I could think of was trying to preserve any water that might possibly come down in a cloudburst.

"I looked around for something—anything at all—to capture rainwater in and I spied a rusty old tin can..."

The man clapped his hand to his forehead. "Of course, I had forgotten about that."

"And I shook it out real good, just to empty out the dirt and pebbles down inside—and out popped this key."

He pulled it out of pocket and held it out in the man's direction.

"Of course I wondered what in the world it was for so I began looking around the framework. And there it was, the locked door leading to this room.

"I do apologize for breaking and entering. I realize this is an unforgiveable invasion of your privacy. But I have to tell you, I've never been so relieved in my life as I was when I opened the door and found this—"

Words failed him at that point and he just sat there for a moment at a complete loss of words.

The other man continued to stare at Dave as if he was trying to make up his mind about something.

He was not tall, but he was well-built, as if he worked out a lot. And there was something commanding about the way he carried himself. He was probably in his thirties, not handsome, but attractive in a rough sort of way. He had several tattoos on the side of his neck, but the most interesting thing about him was his closely-cut dark hair which sported a fade across the back of his head featuring a lightning zigzag.

"Why were you stranded out there?" he asked. "Just out of curiosity, I mean. Did your car break down? Or..." he hesitated a moment. "...or did someone leave you out there like that? And if so—why would they have done such a thing?"

Dave pondered this question a moment before making a quick decision. He was at this guy's mercy now. He was an interesting type, but he seemed reasonable, under the circumstances. Dave decided to tell the truth.

"It was a woman," he said. "She was mad at me and she just dumped me out of the car and went off and left me there. Don't ask me what we were doing out there—sightseeing, I guess. But she got on her high horse and decided I was her worse nightmare.

"She probably had her reasons," he added. "But believe me I didn't deserve to be left out there to die like a rat."

The other man nodded. He had probably had woman trouble, too, at some point in his life. Dave's story sounded entirely plausible to him.

"Okay, David," he said. "I can't blame you for trying to stay alive. That was pretty cold of the lady, stranding you out there without water and all. By the way, my name is Benjamin," he added. "But most people just call me Bennie.

"Now, how can we fix you? I can get you back to civilization all right. I hadn't planned to go back into town right away, of course. But I see your dilemma. You'll need to get back—back to wherever you need to be, I'm guessing. Am I right?"

Dave heaved a sigh of relief. "You've got that so right, Bennie," he said. "And I guess I don't need to tell you how much in your debt I am. I *will* make it up to you—and that's a promise."

"Aw, forget about it," Bennie said. He stepped forward and held his hand out. "Do you need any more sleep or rest? If not, we can get on the road right now."

"I don't need any more sleep, if you're willing to take me now. I'm ready to go any time you are. In fact, the sooner we get going the better, as far as I'm concerned. By the way," he added. "Please call me Dave, like my friends do."

By the time Dave had used the facility again and drank another cold bottle of water at Bennie's insistence, it was already midafternoon.

As they headed out in Bennie's dusty but sturdy ATV, Dave thanked him again for his help.

"That's a great little place you've got there," he said. "Everything is so well thought out and convenient. It must have taken you some time to put it all together."

"No," Bennie said. "It didn't take me so long really, I sort of inherited the place, you might say, from a former business associate of mine. This room had already been carved out but the place was just being used as a storage area of sorts. When I got hold of it I decided to fix it up a bit—make it a truly sustainable off-grid shelter. I might have gotten a bit carried away…"

"Not to my mind," Dave said. "You can't imagine—well, maybe you can—just how I felt when I walked in and that light popped on. I really thought I had died and gone straight to Heaven!"

Bennie chuckled. "Well, now there's a thought. That lady friend of yours would have liked that idea I bet!"

Dave grimaced. He had almost put Carmen out of his mind.

Yes, indeed, he thought. She would have been most relieved at the idea.

Bennie drove steadily and Dave found himself nodding off, although a bit uncomfortably in the ATV passenger's seat. At least the vehicle was enclosed and Bennie had turned the air conditioning on.

He had been able to contact Richard using Bennie's phone once they got into range again and at Bennie's suggestion they agreed to meet up at one of the big name hotels on the Vegas strip just as soon as Richard could arrange a flight from the Bay Area.

"What in God's name happened to you?" The tension was obvious in Richard's voice. "I didn't know where to start looking when I didn't hear from you last night."

"It's a long story," Dave said. "I'll tell you all about it in person. Oh, and the gentleman with me here has been extremely helpful. In fact I might not have made it out of here without his assistance. I am going to need to reward him—in a big way…"

Bennie shook his head "No," but Dave ignored him.

"Understood," Richard said. "You got it, buddy. You have no idea how worried I've been. And that's not all that's been going on either."

"I've got a pretty good idea. I was worried about me, too! As I said, it's a long—and pretty wild—story. Something you're never going to believe. I hope your news is better than mine. What else is going on? Nothing serious, I hope."

Richard paused before answering. There was no point in putting more stress on Dave right now.

"Look," he said. "I'll meet you in Las Vegas just as soon as I can get a plane out of here. We can get caught up on all the news then."

After Dave had hung up, Bennie shook his head again. "I really don't need any reward or anything. You found my place on your own. And now I'm just doing what I would hope someone would do for me—if I ever found myself in that sort of predicament."

"I know," Dave said. "And I appreciate all that. But, trust me. I'm able and glad to do it. And if you don't want to accept anything from me, please just take it and pass it along to someone else who might need it more."

"Now," Bennie said. "That sounds like a plan. I might have just the right place for it, as a matter of fact. I'll have to give it some more thought."

After that, they continued to ride along quietly and companionably until they began hit the main highway.

"It won't be long now," Bennie said. "It should take us no more than an hour or so. I know the people at the hotel there. We'll get a suite and you can take a bath and get cleaned up, if you like, maybe even before your friend arrives."

"I can hardly wait," Dave said. "For the bath, I mean. And I'm also wondering just how decadent I can allow myself to be for dinner this evening. You're welcome to join us, of course."

"We'll see," Bennie replied. "As I said, I have friends there. Maybe we can dream up a really special meal for you. I, for one, think you've earned it!"

* * * *

True to his word, Bennie pulled into the front entrance at one of the major hotels and gambling casinos on the Las Vegas strip just a little over an hour later.

Dave was somewhat taken aback when several attendants rushed out to welcome them and take charge of the car. "Wash, as usual?" one of them said to Bennie.

He nodded. "Yeah, better give it the works. I'll be here for at least a day or so."

Then, as they strolled into the spacious lobby, the manager came forward, his hand out.

"Hi, Bennie," he said. "We didn't expect you back here until next week sometime. I hope everything is all right."

He glanced at Bennie's disheveled companion. "Do you want your usual suite?"

"Yes, we're fine. We've just been out exploring a bit. This is Mr. Spaulding, by the way. He'll be staying in the suite as my guest. We'll have someone else coming in shortly, too. I'd appreciate it if you'd keep an eye out for him. Richard—Black Wolf, isn't it?"

He turned to Dave.

"Yes, that's right," Dave said. "Richard Black Wolf is his full name. And, I'd like the bill to come to me..."

The manager looked at him quizzically, and Bennie laughed out loud.

"That won't be necessary, Dave. I'll explain it to you later. But thanks for the offer, anyway. Oh, and by the way," he added before the manager sped off. "Could you have someone bring up a fresh set of clothes from the hotel shop for Mr. Spaulding?"

The manager, who was introduced to Dave as Gordon, said that he would be glad to do so, and did Mr. Spaulding have a suggestion about sizes and style?

Mr. Spaulding was beginning to understand that there was a lot more to Bennie than he had at first suspected. Clearly, he was a celebrity or frequent guest of sorts and very well known to the management here at this world-class hotel.

He allowed himself to be led docilely to the elevators—and was not surprised, a few moments later, to see that they were being escorted into what was obviously the penthouse suite on the top floor. Las Vegas, in all its glittery glory, was on display through double sets of plate glass windows and doors leading to a wide veranda filled with comfortable lounging furniture.

Twenty-four hours ago, he thought, I was sure I was going to die, alone and in agony, out there on that forsaken desert. Tonight it looks like I'll be wined and dined and treated like royalty.

Easy come, easy go, as they say. It's all in the roll of the dice.

* * * *

Bennie showed Dave into the master bathroom. It was the size of an aircraft hangar---at least that was how it appeared to him.

"Take as long as you want," Bennie told him, laying out a toothbrush and extra toiletries on the spacious marble counter. "Don't worry. Gordon will have people keeping a lookout for your friend. He'll be brought right up as soon as he arrives."

He showed Dave the intricacies of the spa-like bath, then left him alone.

Dave took a long look at himself in the full length mirror. He was a sight all right. Every horrible moment of the past day and a half seemed ground into his bent over stance, his stained and disheveled clothing and, most of all, etched deep into his face and eyes.

He looked, he thought, like something out of some third-rate horror flick. He resembled a monster more than a man. And every bone and muscle in his body ached with protest at all he had asked of them during his ordeal.

He turned the spigots on full blast and immediately hot steamy water began to pour into the roomy contoured tub. He thought a moment then added a dollop of bubble bath sitting nearby. *Why not?* he thought. The masking scent would be a favor to his companions.

When the bubbly steaming hot water had reached the rim he shut off the taps, tested for heat, and gingerly stepped in. As he sank back in ecstasy, he reached to one side and turned on the jets.

He could not believe how much this little bit of luxury meant to him. Was heaven really just privacy and a hot bath?

He could have stayed there all night without a murmur, but discretion told him he needed to get busy washing off the dirt and grime and get out and be ready to greet Richard as soon as he arrived.

Reluctantly, he left the steamy bath and grabbed a terry cloth robe hanging nearby. At least he would be covered, if the new clothing had not arrived yet. But while he was busy brushing his teeth a knock came at the door.

"Are you decent yet?" Bennie called. "I've got your clothes for you. I'll just lay them out here on the bed."

"Thanks. I'll be out in a few minutes."

"Take your time. Your friend is just coming in to the lobby now. I'll get him settled while you're dressing."

He was taken aback when he saw the array of brand-new clothing laid out neatly on the king-size bed. The outfit must have cost hundreds of dollars, if not more. It included a beautiful pair of stylish slacks, what looked to be a hand-crafted coordinating dress shirt, underwear, socks and neat dark loafers. Everything was in the exact sizes he had stated, and it all fit perfectly. Hanging nearby was a casual sport jacket and matching tie.

When he looked in the mirror the next time, he almost did not recognize the dapper gentleman he saw before him.

"There you are!" boomed Richard, as Dave stepped into the living room. "Thank God! What happened to you? I've been worried sick about you."

The two men embraced, and Richard pounded Dave heartily on the back making him cough.

'Whoa there," Dave said. "Take it easy. I'm still pretty stiff and sore."

"Sorry," Richard said. "I just…well, damn it, man. It's a relief to see your ugly mug again. Why didn't you let me know where you were?"

"That is a very long story," Dave replied. "And I'm hungry as hell right now. I haven't had a decent meal for a couple of days." He turned to the other man, standing quietly in the background.

"This is Bennie, by the way. Now, you know the area, Bennie. Is there someplace we can go and grab a bite?"

"That's all right," Bennie said. "I've already introduced myself. And…"

He stepped aside to reveal a dining table already set up with white linen and china in front of the large glass window looking out on the strip.

"Everything's all ready for you and your friend to order whatever you want," he said. "We have a superb kitchen here, and a varied menu. I think you can find something you'll like."

"You've thought of everything," Dave said. He turned to Richard. "This man saved my life. I honestly owe him everything and, as I said before, I'll want to see him compensated."

"That really won't be necessary," Bennie said, shaking his head vigorously as Dave tried to interrupt.

"I've enjoyed meeting you—a lot I might add. And," he paused then grinned. "Actually, I've been having the time of my life. It's been great, seeing my little hideaway up there on the desert being put to some good use for a change. Mostly I check in and out of there once in a while, just to be sure everything is as it should be. I always thought it might come in handy—oh, say, if we had a nuclear disaster or something on that order.

"But to have that little shack actually save someone's life in such a dramatic manner—well, all I can say is, it has been an adventure beyond my wildest dreams."

"Now," he added. "Please go ahead and give your orders to the wait staff. Anything you like. I've got some business to attend to with Gordon and I'll give you two a chance to get caught up."

He held up his hand as Dave started to protest.

"No," he said. "I want you and your friend to feel comfortable to discuss whatever you need to in complete privacy."

So saying, he went to the outer door and gestured in the waiter to take their dinner orders.

"See you later on," he said, heading off toward the elevators.

"Now," said Richard. "We have a lot to talk about."

THIRTEEN

Once she had gotten rid of that stinking piece of garbage known as David Spaulding, Carmen dug in for the long haul. She headed due west of the gleaming dry salt flats and straight into the setting sun, pushing the dusty black Land Rover across the desert terrain toward the mountains for all it was worth.

She didn't slow down until she finally had crossed the border into California and came to a bustling all night truck stop just outside of Yosemite National Park.

She left the vehicle to be filled up and, hoisting the all-important tote which never left her side, headed into the brightly-lit café.

She placed an order for the hot meal special and coffee before visiting the restroom where she took stock of her appearance. Her hair was a mess, and she brushed it smooth with a vengeance before applying fresh makeup and rinsing out her dry mouth under the tap.

Returning to her booth, she ate steadily and ravenously, wiping up the last bit of gravy from her plate with a heel of bread.

"Dessert?" the waitress asked, clearing the dishes and offering a second cup of coffee.

"No, thanks," she said. "But if you could fill my thermos with hot coffee that would be great."

She paid the tab with cash, adding a generous tip, and headed back out to the freshly-fueled car. She had decided to try and make the north shore of Lake Tahoe by dawn, if at all possible. It was about 200 miles, she figured, and doable, if she didn't run into any delays or problems along the way.

As she drove, she kept going over and over her final conversation with David Spaulding. Something about it kept niggling at her brain. Was it something she had said—or done?

The car radio was set on a jazz station and in between sets her mind reviewed, again and again, everything they had said to each other during that final ride—and even more importantly, just what it was she had said to him.

And then it came to her, all of a sudden, like a lightning bolt.

"...*the Mounties always get their man....*"

Why? Why in God's name had she said that? That oh so too revealing Freudian slip that, to a man of Spaulding's intellect, could mean one thing and one thing only—Carmen Ruiz, of Cuban descent, and a native of Miami, Florida—had some kind of recollection or connection with things Canadian!

Whatever had possessed her to lose control over her language at such a pivotal moment? After all the years she had spent learning and practicing her craft and becoming a master at subterfuge and disguise, why, at this specific point in time, did she allow her tongue to go off course and make such a bubble-headed error in judgment?

She tried to comfort herself with the certain knowledge that David Spaulding, whom she had abandoned out on that salt flat, hands and feet bound and with no provisions, especially water, would almost surely die of exposure and thirst. He could be dead already, for all she knew.

And even if—dare she entertain the thought— even if he *did* manage to survive his ordeal, she would be thousands of miles away from their last encounter by then.

With any luck, in fact, she could be back in her native Canada in just a few days..

But if David Spaulding *did* manage to survive his ordeal, she thought nervously, he would begin to put two and two together and, without a doubt, he would surmise that she had fled to Canada. Further, he also knew her present identity as "Carmen Ruiz," the precious identity that she had practically sweat blood and tears acquiring with such care and precision over the past few months.

She thought and thought, as she drove north into the night. What on earth could she do? One thing was for sure. She could not be certain that he would meet his end in the desert.

And if David Spaulding did manage to stay alive—then, almost certainly, the woman known as "Carmen Ruiz" would have to die.

* * * *

When she reached the Lake Tahoe area, just before dawn, she took her time finding a suitable spot to hole up for a few days while she plotted her next course of action. She consulted her phone app for motels and boarding houses, and finally settled on a place called the Bide-Away Inn, located on a two-lane road well off the main highway—and very far away from all the glitz and glitter of the fancy resorts along the Lake's edge.

She pulled into the circular gravel driveway, parked, and entered a quaint, faux-pine-paneled building labeled "Office—Open All Night" in blinking neon lights. The "O" in "Open" was out, however, so the sign read, instead, "Office—pen All Night" which didn't make a lot of sense.

She decided she was too sleepy to judge, however, and once the clerk had shuffled his way from the back room out to the desk in answer to her pinging of the bell, she signed up and paid quickly in cash for three days in a cabin located at the back of the court. Hopefully, the Land Rover could be parked back there, too, somewhat out of view of the highway.

Trundling the tote (which never left her sight), she stumbled along behind the young man, who looked to be as drowsy as she was, until they reached a lonely little bungalow sitting off all by itself at the rear of the property, well out of sight of the outer access road.

As the clerk opened up the door for her, she asked if it would be all right to park behind the trees at the back, and he allowed as how that would be "Okey-dokey," so far as he was concerned.

She took the key from his sweaty palm and immediately headed back out to the front lot to retrieve the car. Once she was safely parked away in the back behind a small copse of raggedy pines, she retrieved all her other bags and hauled everything in to the cottage.

She would leave nothing in the vehicle overnight—and certainly nothing to chance in this godforsaken place.

After double-locking herself in, she made a complete tour of the room, kitchenette, and adjoining bath. Everything looked as if it had been designed and furnished in the 1950s. It also looked like it hadn't undergone a thorough cleaning since that era either. There was dust on the furniture and shelves and several suspicious looking stains on the threadbare carpet. When she pulled down the bedding it looked clean enough, although some sort of bug, suspiciously resembling a flea, jumped out at her. She squished it matter-of-factly and heaved a sigh.

So this place wasn't perfection, in any sense of the word. But it would do for the time being. At least it was secluded, and she had hidden the Land Rover out of sight and away from the street as best she could. With any luck, she could stay here undetected until she could formulate some kind of new plan.

She turned out the light and crawled into bed.

The sun was just coming up over the horizon as she fell into a deep sleep.

* * * *

The very next thing she knew, she heard a light tap-tapping at the cabin door. She bounded out of bed and threw on her clothes before peering out the grimy, grease-streaked front window to see who was demanding entrance.

A young woman dressed in work clothes stood there beside what was obviously a cleaning cart.

"Yes?" she said, opening the door a crack. "What do you want?"

"Sorry, Missy," the girl said. "I didn't know you were asleep. I just wanted to know if you want the sheets changed."

She opened the door a little further and looked the maid over carefully.

"*Venga aqui*," she said, taking a chance.

The girl looked startled at first, but then stepped gingerly across the threshold.

"*Si*...er, yes ma'am."

She was relieved. This one was Hispanic in background. This chance meeting might give her an advantage she hadn't been expecting.

"Come on in," she said, in English this time. "Sit down a minute and let's talk. I think maybe we might be able to do each other some real good."

The girl's full name was Lisa Gonzalez, she said. She was twenty years old and had never been anywhere outside this small roadside community not far from the gambling casinos at Lake Tahoe. Both of her parents had emigrated from Columbia during what they called "the troubles," and both had been working steadily in the thriving hotel and resort industry lakeside since their arrival in the United States.

Lisa, however, had chosen to stay here, rather than follow her parents into a more complicated world. She had not finished high school, nor was that a goal, and cleaning these motel rooms was the first and only job she'd ever held.

"Lisa," Carmen said. "*¡Que bonita!* Would you like a coke?" She gestured at the bar frig chugging away on a counter in the corner.

Lisa shook her head. She didn't know whether to be afraid or intrigued. This beautiful lady was taking such an unusual interest in her, Lisa. No one had ever done that before. In fact, most of the time she was treated more like a piece of furniture than a human being—except, of course, when the local guys were trying to have their way with her.

"Now," Carmen added. "I think we can be *amigas*. Would you like that? I think I can help you. And I think you might be able to help me with some errands I need to run. This might be a very good thing for both of us."

Lisa continued to sit there, silent and dumbfounded. No one had ever spoken to her in this manner. She didn't know what to do or say, but obviously she needed to respond.

"Uh, sure," she said softly. "I could run some errands for you Miss—"

"Oh you can just call me Carmen. There's no need to be formal about it."

"All right, Miss—er, *Carmen*. I would be happy to help with your errands, if you think I can."

The woman known as Carmen pulled a silver ring set with a tiny blue stone off one of her fingers and handed it to the girl.

"Here, Lisa. This is a little gift from me to you, just to seal the deal. Put it on and let's see how it fits."

Nervously, the girl pushed the ring on to the same finger of the same hand and twisted it around. She stared down in awe at the bright blue stone, glinting back at her.

"It's so pretty," she said. "Is it worth a lot of money? I wouldn't want to lose it or harm it in any way while I'm cleaning."

"But I've given it to you. It's yours now, so it doesn't really matter!" Carmen said with a smile, reaching out and patting the girl on the shoulder. "Don't worry about it, Lisa. It's not all that valuable, but I think it looks very pretty on you. It's a gift, *un regalo*, to seal our friendship. The first of many to come, I hope."

So saying, she stood and stretched her arms. "Is there any place close by where we can go grab a bite to eat?" she said. "I'm starving."

And as luck would have it, there *was* a half-way decent little diner just up the road from the Inn.

"I'd rather walk, if it isn't too far from here," Carmen suggested. "I've been cooped up inside the car for far too long. I need some exercise out in the fresh air."

The truth was, she did not want to take the Land Rover out on the road—now that she had it hidden away. But she didn't tell Lisa that.

And so the two women went to the front of the complex and hiked on up the road about half a mile until they came to a Mom-and-Pop place, complete with tableside jukeboxes and pieces of homemade apple pie in a revolving glass display case.

It was something right out of a Norman Rockwell painting Carmen thought, digging into the daily special and chatting about nonsensical girly things with her eager new companion.

"Say," she said, idly stirring her coffee. "I think we must be about the same dress size. I'll bet I have a few clothes that would fit you perfectly. Why don't you come on by the cabin at about the same time tomorrow and I'll have some things out for you to try on. We can do your makeup, and I have some ideas about your hair, too. It'll be fun, I promise you!"

Lisa's eyes glazed over. She felt like she was in some kind of a dream. It was hard to believe all these good things were happening to her.

She smiled back at Carmen. "Oh, gee, I'd really love that!" she said, taking another bite of her pie. "But why are you being so nice to me?"

"Umm, well for one thing," Carmen said. "I never had a little sister, so I feel like I missed something growing up. And, just so this stays something special between us, let's just keep our friendship a secret, shall we? Just between the two of us.

"After all," she added. "We don't want anybody else barging in and spoiling it all, now, do we?"

"No," Lisa said slowly. But, still, she felt just a little bit funny about keeping it a secret. She always told her Mama everything that ever happened to her.

This would be the first time in her life she had kept something this important to herself. She decided she kind of liked the feeling.

* * * *

The very next day, right on time as promised, Lisa showed up at Carmen's door, *sans* cleaning cart.

"I explained to Miz Clary, the owner, that you wanted me to help you out with some errands today," she said. "So Miz Clary, she gave me the day off."

She stood in the doorway, shuffling her feet nervously.

"Well," Carmen said, with an air of disappointment. "That's all right, I guess. But I thought we were going to keep our friendship a secret—just between the two of us."

Lisa responded in horror. "Oh, no, Miss—Carmen! I meant no harm. Honest I didn't!"

"Well, that's all right then. No harm done, I suppose." Carmen tossed her head in disapproval. "But let's not do that again, shall we? This will all work out much better if nobody else knows we're friends."

Lisa shook her head violently. "Oh, I won't tell a soul, Miss—Carmen. I swear I won't!"

"Hmm. We'll see." Carmen gestured. "Well, don't just stand there. Come on in. We have a lot to do today. We'd better get started."

Several hours later, Carmen stood back and studied her handiwork thoughtfully.

The new Lisa resembled nothing like the forlorn little cleaning maid from before. Her hair had been lightened, trimmed, and styled into a reasonable facsimile of Carmen's expert do. Her eyebrows had been plucked and reshaped, and Carmen's own special makeup had been applied expertly, playing up the contours of Lisa's face which most resembled her mentor's creamy complexion.

Even more astonishing, a spare set of contact lenses had been unearthed to render her eye color a riveting shade of blue.

She was now dressed in a smart new pant suit, a stylish blouse, and perky little heels to match. Overall, as the two women stood side by side staring into the big mirror over the bureau, it was difficult, at a glance, to tell one from the other.

"You see," Carmen said triumphantly. "Didn't I tell you? We look just like twins now."

"I can't believe it," Lisa said, quickly wiping away a tear before it could smudge her eye shadow. "I didn't think it was possible."

"And now, my dear," Carmen went on. "Now you owe *me* a big favor. I need you to drive me someplace—not too far away—for a special errand. Do you think you can do that?"

"Well, I've never driven a Land Rover before, but I do know how to drive," Lisa said. She hesitated a moment. "The only problem is—well, I don't have my license yet."

She hung her head in fear. Would this lapse bring their friendship to an early end?

"Oh, that shouldn't be a problem, my dear," Carmen said. "No problem at all. I've got *my* drivers' license—not to mention all kinds of identification. Since you look so much like me now, I see no reason why you can't just carry my ID while you're driving—just in case…"

She didn't add what the "just in case" might entail, but her explanation satisfied Lisa.

"Well, if you think it's all right," she said. "I guess I could do that."

"Good! Now here's what we need to do…"

With that, she outlined the scheme that she had been plotting and planning all through the night. At least she told Lisa the least little part of it she needed to know. It was of vital importance to accomplish all these steps quickly before her nemesis David Spaulding might show his ugly face again.

But it all depended on the timing. If the map she had googled was accurate enough, and if everything else worked out just right—she might yet extract herself from this mess cleanly—and completely.

A short while later, the two women bundled themselves into the front seat of the Land Rover and headed out on to the main highway. Lisa, who was driving, was nervous but determined to prove she could accomplish this task. She ground the gears a couple of times, drove slower than necessary, and kept looking into the rear view mirror to make sure no one was following in her wake.

"You're doing just fine," Carmen kept encouraging her, praying inwardly that Lisa wouldn't do something stupid and spoil the whole scheme.

But a few miles into it, Lisa had visibly relaxed and actually seemed to be enjoying her unexpected outing.

"I always knew I could drive all right," she said. "I just have a little trouble passing the test."

Carmen didn't say anything. She was busy calculating their route, instructing Lisa on when and where to turn, and all the while keeping track of the mileage.

They finally reached a nearly hidden turnoff which led back into a heavily forested area.

"Gee," Lisa said, looking about in concern. "I've never been out this way before. What is this place anyway?"

"Just wait," Carmen reassured her. "You'll see. It's not much further now, and it will all be worth it"

It will be worth it for me, she thought to herself.

Finally they reached a split in the road, which by now was little more than a forest path. Consulting her map again, Carmen pointed to the left. "This way," she said. "It's just around this corner."

Sure enough, as they rounded the curve, the whole forest opened up to a grand vista of mountains and hills and valleys below. The effect was stunning and Lisa drew in her breath in awe.

"It's beautiful," she whispered. "You're right. This was worth the drive." She hesitated, just a moment. "But why are we out here, Carmen? You said there was something we would need to do here. And why was it necessary for me to do the driving? You're a much better driver than I am, I'm sure."

"Oh, I have my reasons," Carmen replied mysteriously. "Now, let's just sit here a minute and take in this gorgeous view. In the meantime," she added. "I've brought along a bite to eat and some coffee. Let's have our lunch, and I'll tell you some more about what I want our future to look like."

So saying, she reached in the back seat and pulled out a sack and a small thermos. Carefully, she laid out their sandwiches and poured them each a cup of steaming coffee.

"Here," she said handing the brew to Lisa. "Drink up now. You earned your reward today!"

Lisa took the hot cup in her two hands, blew and took a sip. "This tastes great," she said. "Thanks, Carmen. You think of everything. This is so much fun! It feels like we're on a picnic!"

"I thought it would be," Carmen said, busying herself with napkins. She waited a moment while Lisa finished her first cup. "Shall I pour you another?"

When Lisa nodded and held out her cup, Carmen filled it up again. "Now, why don't you relax a little bit and enjoy this fine view. Let's talk about the future."

"I just want to thank you so much, Carmen," Lisa began. "You've been so kind to me. Nobody has ever treated me this way before."

She babbled on and on then, as she nibbled at her sandwich and sipped her coffee. She was enthusiastic and felt herself being garrulous far beyond her normal behavior around strangers.

And as she talked, she began waving her hands around, gesturing wildly—first at Carmen—then at the stupendous scenery in front of them.

The older woman did not respond, at first. Then, as Lisa began to flail about, knocking over the remaining dregs of her coffee and scattering the remains of her half-eaten sandwich across the seat and floor of the car, Carmen reached out, grabbed Lisa's arm and shouted at her.

"Shut up, you little bitch!"

Lisa blinked and stopped moving. A trace of spittle appeared at the corner of her mouth, and she gasped for air. "Wha—?" she began.

"You stupid girl," Carmen said, still holding her with an iron grip. "Why in the world would you think I'd ever want to have anything to do with the likes of you?

"Now let me tell you what's really about to happen. The coffee you just drank and that sandwich you just ate were doctored. They were full of poison and you, my girl, you're about to die—Yes, you are going to *die*!" she emphasized, as Lisa began to whine, eyes wide and uncomprehending.

"And once you've expired, as you surely will, in just a matter of minutes now—once that happens, I'm going to start up this car, aim it toward that mile-high canyon over there, and send you over the cliff.

"With any luck, the car will blow up on impact and your body will be burned beyond recognition. Also, with further luck, there will be a few pieces of Carmen Ruiz's identification left intact. And, for a while at least, I will be dead—and able to start over completely, in a new place, and as somebody else."

"Aieee!" Lisa screamed, trying desperately to free herself from Carmen's firm grasp. "But why? Why *me*?"

"Because you came along at just the right moment," Carmen said. "You were the next best thing to me. That's the only reason why. It was just a happy accident."

Lisa began flailing less and less now. Carmen watched her, unemotionally, remembering the final movements of the fledgling bird as it lay dying on the deck of Larry's boat in the Caribbean.

It should only be a few more minutes at the most now. And then she would be free—once more.

When all Lisa's movements had ceased, Carmen reached over and checked the girl's pulse—just to be sure.

Then she gathered up all the evidence, the sandwiches, the now empty thermos, and Lisa's lipstick-stained cup, and stuffed it all back down into the lunch bag. Next she went through Lisa's purse, making sure to remove all of the identification pertaining to her and leaving only the drivers' license, Social Security, passport and other miscellaneous ID cards in the name of Carmen Ruiz.

She also wiped down what she could of any of the miscellaneous fingerprints the two of them might have left in the car. This latter step was just an unnecessary precaution, she hoped. But she tried to be thorough all the same.

Getting out the passenger side, she went around to the rear and removed her ever-present tote bag and another small carry-on containing a change of clothes and just a few necessities and set them out by the edge of the trail. What was left of Carmen's clothing was all stashed neatly into several other bags she deliberately left in the back of the car.

She hated to lose them, but they could have no place in her next incarnation.

She glanced around, then bent down and picked up a sizeable chunk of granite. Opening the driver's door, she leaned over Lisa's inert body, switched on the engine, and plopped the heavy rock down on top of the accelerator pedal.

The engine roared to life. Checking one more time to make sure Lisa's seat belt was secure and the direction of the steering wheel seemed on target, Carmen released the emergency brake, quickly backed out of the car, and slammed the door shut.

With the accelerator held down to the floor, the Land Rover sprang forward with a mighty leap—rapidly traversing the short distance to the edge of the cliff and then, in a slow motion arc reminiscent of Thelma and Louise, Carmen's car sailed out and over the chasm below.

It was all over in a very few minutes. Somewhere toward the bottom of the canyon, she could hear the *clunk, clunk, clunk* of metal hitting rock as Lisa and her chariot drifted toward eternity.

She stood at the top of the cliff and looked down on chaos. The Land Rover lay on its back in ruins, wrecked to smithereens. As she watched and waited—and just as she had hoped, an ominous black stream of smoke appeared.

A few minutes later there was a loud *Pop* and tongues of flame began snaking their way upward, one by one, ravenously seeking out the life-giving fuel leaking from the now useless gasoline tank lying trapped within the wreckage.

Boom!

And then it was all over. As Lisa and the Land Rover went up in smoke, the woman once known as Carmen turned back down the hill.

* * * *

She checked her map again, gathered her bags, and headed on foot back down the hill the way they had come. A mile or so down the track she spotted a faint hiking trail veering off toward the east.

It took her nearly an hour to reach her destination, but the narrow path was well-shaded and every so often she came upon a bench or a large boulder where she could pause and catch her breath.

Eventually she broke out on to the main access road. She checked her bearings again before turning right, to head south and back in the direction of the motel. Another mile further, around a bend and just as the map had shown, the same little diner where she and Lisa had eaten the day before popped into view.

She practically cheered out loud, but refrained from showing any emotion at all, as she casually opened the door and stepped inside.

"Oh, hi there," called out the waitress from behind the counter. "You were in here yesterday, weren't you? Where's your friend?"

"She couldn't make it today," the woman once known as Carmen said. "She had to go out of town this morning. She said she was headed up north somewhere. It was a family emergency I think."

"Oh, that's a shame. You two girls looked like you were having such a good time together." She paused, coffee pot in hand. "Have a seat in that front booth over there. Can I get you something to eat?"

"No. I'm not here for anything to eat. I'm looking to catch that daily bus down to the casino. Do you know what time it stops here?"

"Oh, sure. It should be by in about half an hour or so. Do you want a round trip ticket?"

"No," she said. "I'll just need a one way. My folks work down there. They called this morning and said they might have a job for me. So I guess I'll go see what it is."

The woman squinted at her. "Oh, you must be *Lisa*, then. You and your friend look so much alike I couldn't be sure. Yeah, I don't blame you. That sounds like it might be a great opportunity for you."

She busied herself at the cash register for a minute before handing the woman now known as Lisa a stamped ticket.

"Here it is. Go ahead and sit down. You can wait in here if you like. Are you sure you don't want a cup of coffee or something—on the house? "

"Thank you," she said. "That's very kind of you but I think I'll go on outside until the bus comes. After all, I don't want to miss my ride."

She took a seat on the bench just beyond the front door of the café and settled in to wait. Sure enough, just as the waitress had promised, about twenty minutes later a dusty Greyhound pulled into the graveled parking lot and opened its doors with a wheeze.

The woman once known as Carmen but now known as Lisa climbed aboard the bus and gave her one-way ticket to the driver. She found an empty seat in the back and stowed her bags right up next to her, near the window, so they couldn't be rifled or stolen should she fall asleep.

After all, she thought, you really couldn't be too careful these days. There were a lot of crazy people out there.

* * * *

"Cash," she said. "And I have to have current tags and a pink slip."

The manager eyed her cautiously.

She wasn't his typical customer. Most of the people he dealt with were gamblers down on their luck trying to unload their vehicles for enough to stake them for another run at the cards, or the dice—or whatever their particular addiction happened to be.

"Well," he said, trying to gauge how much she was good for. "Just what kind of vehicle did you have in mind, now? We've got your basic transportation cars—or," he paused a moment, wondering if he had a live one on the line. "Or, if you'd be at all interested, we have a couple of really high-end babies—the cream of the crop, so to speak.

"Just tell me what you're looking for."

She pulled out the roll of $1,000 bills she had already put together before walking from the bus stop to this fly-by-night car lot just off the strip from the Crystal Bay casino.

"Here," she said, plunking her stash down on the counter. "I want the most reliable transportation on the lot—with all the necessary paperwork to go with it. That's my bottom line right there in front of you. Tell me what you can do and I'll decide if that's good enough to meet my needs."

He was already counting it out, using a wetted thumb to separate the bills. When he had finished he pulled out a printed list and began comparing some of the serial numbers at random, just to be sure he wasn't dealing with a forger.

He then jotted down a few numbers on a pad, pulled out another list and scanned it for any vehicles on the lot that were clean, legal, and ready to go.

"I've got one or two possibilities," he said. "Let's go out and take a look."

She followed him out to the lot and on to the line. Referring back and forth to the list in his hand, he pointed out the product he thought matched her specs best.

"Now, this one..." he began....

"No," she said. "That one is too flashy. I don't want anything that's going to draw a lot of attention."

"Okay," he said, a bit disappointed that he wasn't going to be able to unload that bright red Thunderbird he'd paid too much for just yet.

"Now here's one that might be more like what you're looking for."

He stood back and gestured toward a Toyota Camry light gray in color. It wasn't brand new, but it wasn't real old, either. It was clean, it had no obvious dents, and the upholstery looked intact.

He turned the key for her and she checked the panel lights, knowing full well that it would be a complete waste of time to rely on the mileage number. She looked under the hood, could see no evidence of oil or water leakage, and there weren't any odd smells. When she opened the trunk, it was clean and empty except for the car jack.

"Could you throw in an emergency repair kit?" she asked.

"Of course," he said.

"And you can give me a pink slip?" She had already checked the tags and they were current.

"Yes, everything is up to date and kosher on this one." He remembered the guy he bought it from two or three days ago, a high roller heavily addicted to gambling and willing to sell his transportation for a song to feed his habit.

"Believe me," the manager assured her. "You're not going to have any problems with this one."

"Fine," she said. "I'll take it. I'll wait for the paperwork."

"Oh," she added. "And I'd appreciate it if you'd throw in a full tank of gas while you're at it."

The manager escorted her back to the office, scurried around getting the paperwork in order, and ordered the lot man to fill up the gas tank.

"Don't forget that emergency kit," she said. "I don't want to get stuck out on the road somewhere."

An hour later, the woman now known as Lisa Gonzalez was skimming her way north on I-267 toward Truckee where she would spend the night recalibrating her travel plans.

As she drove she went over and over again, everything that had happened since the cruise ship disaster. Somewhere, somehow, she had made mistakes. Still, she could not see how she could have done things any differently.

And she still did not know where David Spaulding fit in to the grand scheme of things.

The uppermost question in her mind was how in the world had he tracked her to California? But he must have done. She could see no other answer beyond pure serendipity. And, as she was fond of saying, she simply did not believe in coincidence. It had to be part of some plot he had designed to trap her and bring her to justice.

But why was he also so concerned about the unknown arsonist who had no ties to her? And his connection to Hightower seemed suspicious as well.

It was all very unsettling. And now that she had scuttled the persona of Carmen Ruiz, would he be able to see through that ruse as well?

But she was forgetting something. There was still a very good possibility that David Spaulding had not survived the ordeal in Death Valley. That was her main hope right now and she clung to it. If her new alias as Lisa Gonzalez held for a time at least she might still be able to make it north to Spokane and then across the border where she could disappear into the hinterlands.

By the time she reached Truckee she was exhausted, both mentally and physically. She searched and found a small group of cabins off the main drag, checked in, and collapsed on the bed. She hoped to get a good night's sleep and make some more detailed plans the next morning.

But sleep failed her. She tossed and turned most of the night as she reviewed over and over all the steps she had taken and where everything had gone wrong.

And she could still hear David Spaulding's voice as if he were right there in the room with her, speaking in her ear.

If we committed an evil act in our past life, we must pay for it in our present existence. By the same token, if we did a good deed in the past, we are sure to reap the benefit in the present.

What was it he had been talking about? Oh, yes. She remembered. It was the concept of karma and how it could be either good or bad. In her case, she supposed, it would have to be bad karma.

There seemed to be no other choices left to her.

The next morning she checked out and found a diner. She ate a quick breakfast and had her thermos filled with coffee.

"I'm headed over to Redding," she said to the waitress. "Can you give me any idea on the best route?"

"Oh, yeah," the girl said. "I'd head straight up to Downieville and across on highway 49. That will take you right on in to Yuba City and Redding is just above there."

As soon as she got back to the car, she plugged the directions in to her GPS and headed out. She felt cranky and tired, but at least she was headed in the right direction. When she reached the Oregon border she figured it would take her at least another two to three days of straight driving to Spokane. But once there, she could breathe easy.

Then, using Lisa's citizen identification card, she only had to walk across the border at Grand Forks and go to ground.

David Spaulding would never find her there.

FOURTEEN

Carl Frick's experiences had started out a lot less stressful than the ordeal his old pals Chip and Dave had been enduring.

The assignment he pulled was in an area not that far from Richard's apartment in San Francisco and even closer than that to the State Forestry headquarters in Sacramento.

At least, he reasoned, he should be able to get assistance in a hurry should he require it.

The fire in question had been burning for several days in Nevada County, which was only about an hour's drive northeast of Sacramento. The authorities were calling it nearly contained, which was a good thing.

But the crews working on mop up had not been able to find a point of origin—nor could they say if it was arson-related.

There was a very good possibility the initial spark had been caused by lightning, given the frequency of rain squalls in the area. But on the off chance the initiator was determined to be more sinister, Carl had been dispatched to the site to make his own investigation—just in case something odd like the man-made cones turned up.

Nevada County was the gateway to a string of historical mining and logging communities which stretched eastward from California's central corridor through the Sierra Nevada mountain range to the Nevada border. Towns like Grass Valley and Nevada City had existed for over a hundred years since the Gold Rush era—and each had its own tale to tell of the havoc left behind by the devastating seasonal wildfires

The current blaze had started somewhere in the woods down along the Yuba River near the little town of Downieville. The area was popular and flooded with tourists during the summer months into fall. Any number of things could have started the fire, including someone being careless about putting out a campfire or the backfire from a car along the highway.

Carl headed out of Grass Valley along Highway 49. His goal was Downieville, but he was prepared to be stopped anywhere along the way and turned back.

If that happened, he would simply backtrack down to Nevada City or any other likely spot. There were numerous diners and bars along this route, and he could make a stab at talking to the locals while getting a meal and deciding his next move.

He was surprised—and relieved—to find that all barriers along the route had been lifted, and cars were once more being allowed through to Downieville and points beyond without restriction.

He stopped at one intersection and spoke with a Highway Patrol team parked alongside the road.

"Is there any news about the fire?" he asked. "I was afraid I might not be able to drive through this area."

"It looks as if they will be calling it contained before too much longer," the officer answered. "We're still asking people to be cautious and not wander off into the woods just yet. These wildfires can be tricky—especially if the winds pick up.

"All the same," he added. "We're hoping this is the end of this one. Of course, the fire crews will be going through the whole area, mopping up and making sure nothing gets started again."

Carl thanked him for the information and headed on in to Downieville. He planned to have dinner there and spend the night if he could find a vacant room. In the morning he would nose around a bit to see if he could find a way in to the point of origin.

That might be kind of tricky, given he was not supposed to reveal his official connections. But still, he could make a try for it.

That evening he found a surprisingly good steak house which seemed popular with the locals. He took his time, enjoying his meal and conversing with a few of the other patrons.

The consensus seemed to be that the worst of the fire was over with and once the mop up had put down all the embers and possible sparks, the crews could pack up and go home to a well-deserved rest.

"It's been pretty bad all over the state," one man commented. "Makes you wonder about all this climate change stuff they keep talking about. I know it's been a lot dryer over the last few years."

"Aw, that's just a bunch of hooey," someone else spoke up. "It's not any worse than most other years, far as I can tell."

Carl deliberately steered clear of the controversy.

"Can anyone tell me if we're allowed to drive down to any of the Yuba River sites yet," he said, to no one in particular. "I'd sure like to get in some fishing while I'm here. I drove all the way up from the Bay Area just to enjoy the scenery and the mountains. I'd hate to go back without getting a chance at that."

"Well," one of the older men said. "If you don't mind a bit of a rough drive, there is a way down to the River that's off the main road. I could draw you a little map if you like."

"Would you?" Carl said. "That would be great. Like I said, I'd just like to see the place. I've heard such great things about the Yuba."

"Sure," the man said. "My name's Al, by the way. If you've got a pen and paper handy, I'll draw it out for you."

Half an hour later, after buying Al another drink, Carl paid his bill, shook hands, and departed back to his motel room.

"Richard," he said a few minutes later. "I'm in a place called Downieville, and I've just lucked in to a way in to the Yuba site. I'm going to...."

"Carl," Richard said. "I've got some news I don't think you're going to want to hear."

Carl's heart fell.

"What's wrong?" he asked. But he didn't really want to hear the answer.

"We haven't had any communication from Chip since he headed out on assignment. I was hoping maybe you might have heard something..."

"No," Carl said. "You and the guy at headquarters in Sacramento are the only people I've talked to over the last two days. What do you think has happened? Should I come back?"

Richard thought a minute.

"No. I think you'd better stay where you are and continue working on your assignment. In the meantime, Everett Hightower and I will start beating the brush to see if we can figure out where Chip is. We know where he was headed. He just hasn't checked in yet.

"There might be nothing to it," Richard added. "At least that's what I'm hoping."

"What about Dave?"

There was a long silence.

"Well, that's just it, Carl. I haven't heard from him either—not since yesterday evening. He might just be delayed in getting back to me. He didn't have anything particularly risky on his agenda for today. That is—"

"What is it, Richard? Do you think there might be something wrong with Dave, too? That's it. I'm shutting down and I'll catch the next flight back down to San Francisco. If either of them is in trouble, I want to be where I can do something to help.

"I understand," Richard said. "But let's give it one more day before you do anything. I'll keep trying to make contact with them. If I don't have any news by tomorrow then yes, by all mean, come on back."

They left it that way and Carl spent most of the night wide awake and worrying about his friends.

Where the hell could they be? And what might have gone wrong? This whole thing had started as a lark and had turned into a nightmare.

What in God's name had they been thinking?

Carl stumbled out of bed the next morning, stopped in the diner for some black coffee, then hurried out to his car. He had studied the little map Al had drawn for him the night before and thought he could find the trail down to the river without too much difficulty.

It was a beautiful day, but there were still ominous black smudges in the sky where the fire had either not yet dissipated or—in a worst case scenario—had flared up again.

Carl had been oblivious to the attractive woman sitting alone in the next booth at the diner. If he had been paying attention at all he would have noticed her staring at him as if she knew him. But his mind was on other things.

The woman, on her part, was transfixed. In fact, she could hardly believe her eyes at first. It had taken her only a moment to recognize the man at the next table as one of several who had been frequent companions of David Spaulding on the cruise ship *Nerissa*.

She didn't remember his name, if she had ever known it, but there was no doubt in her mind that he had been on that ship—and he had been one of Spaulding's closest associates.

He didn't seem to take any note of her however. After a brief visit to the men's room, he finished his coffee, paid the waitress and left the restaurant. She waited a few minutes before following him out to the parking lot.

She watched as he got into his car and quickly made her way over to her own parked nearby. It might be making a gigantic mistake, but her curiosity had gotten the better of her. She *must* know why he was here and if it had anything at all to do with David Spaulding.

As Carl Frick turned out of the diner and back on to Highway 49, a gray Toyota was right behind him. His mind was on other things and he never noticed it at all.

* * * *

The little parade headed southwest on the highway toward Nevada City. Carl's intention, as he glanced at Al's little hand-drawn map, was to find Goodyears Bar, the spot indicated where a walkable trail inclined down from the road toward the North Fork of the Yuba River.

It was just a few miles out of Downieville when he began watching anxiously for signs of the spot. As he drove, he began to feel slightly dizzy and disoriented. Finally, at a wide spot in the road, he pulled over and parked. It took him a moment or two to figure out how to cut the engine.

He lay back in the seat, panting and sweating profusely. It must have been something he ate at the diner, he surmised. Damn! What a time to come down with a classic case of food poisoning.

As he sat there, growing more and more concerned about his condition, he began wondering if he would be able to get the car moving again. Even worse, he began doubting he would be able to find his way down the road if he could get the vehicle started.

In his anxiety about what was happening to him, he failed to notice the gray car that had passed him then turned around and came back to park on the other side of the street heading back to Downieville.

He looked up when he heard a rapping on the window next to his face. Confused as he was, it took him a moment or two to figure out how to lower the damned contraption.

"Are you all right?" The woman was staring down at him. She didn't seem particularly concerned. Still, he was grateful for what he assumed to be an offer of assistance.

"I—I think I might have a touch of ptomaine," he said. "I don't know—don't know what else it could be." He was stammering and even his own voice sounded hollow and tinny in his ears.

"Why don't you come with me," she said. "My car is right across the street. We can go back up to Downieville—see if we can find you a doctor."

He hesitated. Some little worm of caution was niggling away at the back of his brain. Something Richard had said during their most recent conversation.

All of a sudden he had it!

In a burst of self-preservation, he reached through the window and grabbed her arm in what he hoped was a vice grip.

"Not so fast," he gasped. "I know who you are. Did you think I actually drank that coffee you spiked back at the diner?"

She screamed and brought down his wrist hard on the top of the window. The pain forced him to let go. She glanced back at the street and before he could react, she had dashed back across towards her car.

Carl started to open his door to give chase but a loud blare caught him off guard. He stopped just in time to watch a big semi go by him, headed in the direction of Nevada City.

He waited until it had passed and started to open the door again when a gray shadow also whizzed by in the wake of the truck. She had used the opportunity to start her car, whirl around with screeching tires in the middle of the street, and follow after the semi.

She speeded up and went around the truck on a blind curve.

The driver beeped his horn again and shook his fist at her. Damn stupid bitch! What if a car had been coming in the other direction on the two-lane highway? There would have been a bloody accident—and bloody hell to pay, too—if he didn't get his load over to the Coast on time. He would have been held up for hours, if not days. And what would have become of his bonus then?

Carl watched the whole incident and thought hard.

Would he be better off calling it in and waiting for assistance from the authorities? He had, after all, taken a few sips of the coffee before spitting it back.

The aftertaste of whatever she had slipped in it while he was in the restroom had stopped him from swigging down the whole cup. He recalled he had immediately stuffed his paper napkin down into the half-full mug before leaving the diner.

She must have been watching him the whole time and probably assumed he had drained it all in one gulp. That one assumption may have saved his life.

God only knew what would have transpired if he had actually drunk the whole thing. If it was potent enough to make him this nauseated and foggy, the full dose probably would have rendered him completely helpless and unable to put up any sort of defense.

He dug out an anti-acid and crunched it down. He sat there another fifteen minutes or so and felt slightly better. He still had not decided what his next move should be.

Would the woman go on to her next destination and disappear undercover again? Or would she go to ground somewhere up the road, hoping to catch him unawares and run him down—or blow him up, or—what?

Carl had no idea what to expect from his attacker. All he knew for sure was that the lady was crazy and dangerous as hell.

Finally he started the motor and eased back out on to the highway. He drove slowly and cautiously, peering into the underbrush along both sides of his route, prepared at any moment to gun the motor and evade any threat.

Gradually, as he neared the vicinity of Goodyears Bar, he relaxed a bit and began watching for the sign of the trail head outlined on Al's primitive map. At the very least, he could get down near the river, have a look around for anything suspicious, and at least be able to report something back to the others.

He nearly passed it by, the opening was so hidden by brush and straggling pines. But there it was, pretty much as Al had drawn it. The turn off and small gravel parking area were hidden back in the trees. He pulled in, parked, and sat there a moment, taking stock of the location.

The trail heading down the hillside toward the river looked to be easy enough. It wound back and forth between large boulders and trees. It was actually pleasant, hiking along, the sun stippling through the leaves with hints of a bright blue sky peaking in between the larger branches.

He almost began humming a little tune to himself as he planned in his mind what he would do once he reached his goal. First he would look the whole area over, search, as always, for any sign of the tell-tale cones, and keep an eye out for a point of origin for the earlier fire.

Already he was seeing signs of the damage done. The air still reeked of smoke and more and more of the brush and smaller saplings were singed, and in some cases only blackened sticks remained, pointing up to the heavens above in silent condemnation.

"Who the hell are *you*?" a voice growled suddenly as he turned a corner near the bottom of the trail.

Standing there, in a semi-threatening manner, was a man in Forestry gear.

"Sorry," Carl said. "I didn't mean to startle you. I'm just trying to get down closer to the river. I wanted to see for myself what the damage looks like. Somebody in town told me about this trail. I thought the fire had been contained."

"It's not contained until we *say* it's been contained," the man said. "Don't you idiots know how dangerous it is to come into these locations while we're still mopping up?"

Something about the man's attitude got to Carl. His earlier experience with the woman had left him in a belligerent mood, and he spoke up without thinking.

"Look," he said. "Last time I checked, this is a free country. There were no warning signs or law enforcement officers up there telling me I couldn't come down here and check out the site. If you have the authority to tell me to move on, fine. But I think I need to see some paperwork first."

He stuck his jaw out and visibly dared the guy to make him move out.

The man pulled out his ID and shoved it in Carl's face.

"There," he said. "Satisfied now? I suggest you move on before I call the cops."

Carl looked at the card carefully, memorized the name, handed it back, and without thinking too much further about it, hauled out his own ID, the special one he had been warned not to show to just anyone.

"Here," he said. "As you can see, I've got just as much reason to be checking out this area as you do. I'm on special assignment from the U.S. government. So maybe it's you who needs to clear out. And by the way, I'd check my attitude if I were you. Aren't you supposed to be a public servant, not the other way around?"

The only thing the fire fighter needed to see on Carl's government ID was the word "Pittsburgh" as part of his background credentials.

He clocked the interloper with a clenched fist on the side of the head. Carl, still fighting off the after effects of the sedative the woman had slipped him, fell flat on his back. He tried to rally, but by then, his assailant had grappled a rope over and around his neck like a noose.

"Any move," the man warned him, "and I'll tighten this up and break your damned windpipe. Stay down there now and behave yourself while I try to figure out what the hell I'm going to do about you."

Carl did as he was told and laid back quietly on the hard ground, trying to think how best to defuse the situation. He watched the man carefully, hoping he would be distracted enough to allow Carl an opportunity to either get at his cell phone or manage somehow to free himself.

But after a moment, the attacker grabbed the end of the rope and brought it down around Carl's wrists and ankles, leaving him trussed up and immobile.

"There," he said. "That should take care of you for a while."

The man moved back to the sandy edge of the clearing and returned to whatever he had been doing when Carl had interrupted him.

Carl couldn't see clearly from his position, but it appeared to him that the man was digging and then moving something into a small hole.

The cone, he thought. *The guy is making one of the cones. He's the arsonist—and now I know his name!*

A few minutes later, the fireman stood up and looked back over at Carl, who quickly relaxed his body and closed his eyes, as if he had passed out.

He came over and flicked Carl's cheek with his finger. Carl used every ounce of will power to resist flickering, even an eyelash.

"Good," the man grunted. "Out like a light. You're not going to cause any trouble—and you'll never know what hit you."

Carl's heart was pounding like a sledge hammer against his ribs. He could only pray that the sound coming across so loudly in his own ears was not audible to his assailant. He lay as still as he could, breathing shallowly, and willing his hands and feet not to twitch.

The man grabbed something bright and shiny from his gear bag and marched to the side of the clearing that had not yet been touched by fire. He looked up at the sky, and began moving the object around in his hands, trying first this way and then that to get the right angle.

What in the world—? Carl didn't dare look directly at the man. He sensed his very life depended on staying "out cold" for now. Still, even in his position, he was able to peek through half-closed eyelids and get some idea of what was happening.

And then he realized exactly what it was the man was holding so reverently in his hands. It was a magnifying glass—the big kind that older people sometime use to read fine print in documents.

No wonder they could never seem to find an accelerant. The fire starter this arsonist was using was the sun itself!

He could hear the guy muttering to himself as first a wisp of something resembling steam grew into smoke—something about the direction of the blaze. All of a sudden he saw that the trajectory of the new fire would almost certainly head towards him. If he couldn't extricate himself before the conflagration grew into an uncontrollable holocaust, he would be caught straight in its path.

As he pondered all this the smoke thickened and began to turn black. And then tiny tongues of yellow-orange flame flickered and grew, lapping at the dry brush and leaves the man was piling up before it. Twigs were added, and finally, a felled sapling was dragged across the mess as well.

The arsonist stood and watched his handiwork as it grew and grew and began to reach out for more tinder to feed its hungry soul.

"That's enough," he said at last. "That should do the job."

He took one last look at his victim, hogtied on the ground, and now in the very path of the flames.

"See you in hell," he said cheerfully, turning around and heading south through the trees.

Carl watched him out of sight through lidded eyes, thinking all the time, "At least I know who you are, you bastard."

FIFTEEN

As soon as they had gotten word from Everett Hightower about Chip's narrow escape David Spaulding and Richard Black Wolf bid an immediate farewell to their host, Bennie, promising to stay in touch. They then hired a private jet to fly them from McCarran Field in Las Vegas to San Bernardino International Airport at the site of the old Norton Air Force Base.

Once there, they drove straight to Forest Service headquarters a short distance away and were greeted there by an enthusiastic Everett Hightower and a much chastened Chip, who apologized over and over again for not sticking to protocol.

"None of that matters now," Dave said. "At least you're all right. And it sounds as if you have a pretty good idea about who our arsonist might be. That's important information, and I'm not sure we could have gotten it any other way."

"I can't say for sure," Chip said. "But I think it must be one of two people. I hadn't met them before I went up to Camp Seely, but they both seemed to know you pretty well from your operations here in San Bernardino.

"In fact, the one big mistake I seemed to have made was saying I was from Pittsburgh. That really seemed to set them both off."

"Hah!" Richard erupted.

Dave looked uncomfortable. "Really?" he said. "Just that word alone?"

"That's the word the guy whispered in my ear when he shoved me over into Heart Rock Cavern," Chip said. "Swear to God, although I know that sounds nuts."

Dave thought back to his first foray into the Waterman Canyon fire scene.

"Yeah," he admitted. "I guess I made some references to Pittsburgh as being my home base when I first met the fire fighters—and Carmen."

"Now, what's all this about Carmen—and what the hell happened to you in Death Valley? Bring me up to date?"

"Well," Dave said. "You see..."

"I don't think Dave is ready to talk about all that just yet," Richard said. "At least, I think he needs a 'cooling off' time to think about it."

Ev Hightower looked at Richard. "That may well be, Richard," he said. "But I just received some further information that I think you both need to hear. And it may come as something of a shock."

"What's happened now?" Dave said. "If that woman has done any further damage…"

"Easy," Richard said, putting a hand on Dave's shoulder. "Let's hear what Ev has to say. We need to have every piece of the puzzle now, before we can move forward."

Everett glanced back and forth between the two men then cleared his throat.

"Well," he said. "I hate to be the one to give you this news. And I have no idea how you're going to take it. But it looks very much as if one Carmen Ruiz drove her car off a cliff up near Lake Tahoe. It blew up in flames—and it doesn't look like there's—I don't think there's too much left."

There was a long silence. Richard watched Dave carefully, trying to gauge how he was taking the news.

"What proof is there—of her death, I mean," he said finally. "Did they find her body?"

"Yes," Ev said. "At least there was a woman's body in the driver's seat. It had been pretty much burned beyond recognition, but all of the items in the car, whatever ID and clothing they found—all of it appeared to belong to Carmen. Of course, they can try to do a DNA test at some point, but…"

"It isn't her," Dave said. "I'd stake my life on it—again," he said ruefully, glancing at Richard. "My guess is that she didn't trust that I would die in Death Valley and that I would come after her if I survived. She made a couple of mistakes during our conversations, and I think I know a lot more about her than she intended to let slip.

"My hunch tells me that she found some poor girl she duped into getting into the car with her, then killed her and shoved her over the cliff after switching identification. I'll bet she's still heading north, under a new name."

"Why north?" asked Chip.

"I think she's going to head back home—to Canada," Dave said. He explained the slip ups she'd made. "Every time she said something like that she looked odd—as if she realized what a mistake she had made. It got so I could tell when she was lying to me—just by that look on her face."

"Do you think it's worth pursuing her?" Ev said. "After all, she was an employee of the State. It seems to me she'd be liable for some sort of malfeasance in her job, not to mention the murderous assault she made on you."

"My personal reaction is yes, pursue her by all means," Dave said. "If we don't stop her she'll be over the border into Canada within a few days—and I doubt we'll ever find her there.

"On the other hand," he added. "First and foremost, we *must* find and stop the arsonist. That has been our charge from the beginning. My personal grievances should take a second seat to the matter at hand."

"I tend to agree with Dave," Richard said. "The woman is a genuine threat to society—there's no doubt about it. But we've been charged with finding and stopping an unknown arsonist. We didn't think we could do it, but thanks to Chip's bravery and fortitude we now have a very firm lead. This man may not be the only arsonist in the State. But if we can find and stop him, at least California will be a little bit safer."

A vote was taken and all hands agreed. Their first and most important task was to find and stop the arsonist. Carmen could be dealt with later.

Everett Hightower ordered new travel vouchers for all of them, including himself.

"I'm not going to stay behind on this one," he said. "I want to be in there for the kill when we get this son-of-bitch."

* * * *

Once they were all buckled in to the Forestry plane and headed for Sacramento, Richard found an opportunity for a private talk with Dave.

"Are you all right?" he said. "I mean are you really okay after that horrendous experience? We haven't had much of a chance to talk about what happened to you since your rescue.

"That had to have been a harrowing trek," he added. "I'm not sure I would have come through it as well as you did."

Dave nodded. "I don't think I've had enough time to take it all in yet," he said. "I've been so focused on what we're doing here I haven't given much thought to all of the ramifications of my interactions with Carmen.

"I think now I was a bit foolish," he said. "I thought just because I am a man and physically stronger a mere woman couldn't take advantage of me.

"Obviously I was completely wrong about that," he added with a chuckle. "If ever anyone was put in his place, it was me. I have learned a very important lesson, I think. Never take anything or anyone for granted—even with the best intentions."

"After this is all over with," Richard said. "I'd like you to spend some time out here with me, if at all possible. I think it would be good for both of us, just to wind down, have some meaningful conversations and the like.

"Besides," he added. "I'm going to need some expert advice on the details of the new book I have in mind. I think you might be the right person to provide that insight."

"That sounds great," said Dave. "But I'll have to see what the government has to say about it—if I still have a job after this is all over."

He laughed again. "It wouldn't surprise me if they tell me to get on back to Pittsburgh and forget about all this."

Chip was snoozing and Everett was tapping away at his phone. He looked up suddenly.

"Have either one of you heard anything from Carl?" he said. "I've been trying to contact him, but there's been no response since early this morning and his vehicle tracking device doesn't seem to be switched on. I keep thinking he'll check in at any moment, but his handler in Sacramento hasn't been able to raise him either."

"No," said Richard. "I haven't heard a thing from him today. Do they think he might be in trouble?"

"They have no idea. His last message to both of us was that he was going to head out from Downieville early this morning to examine what he thought might be the point of origin site for the Yuba River fire near a place called Goodyears Bar. He had gotten some kind of map from one of the locals he was going to try and follow."

"Is there any way we can divert this flight straight up to that area?" Dave said.

"Let me ask them," Ev said. "I'll see if it's possible."

A little later Hightower confirmed that Forestry headquarters in Sacramento had agreed to divert their flight to the Nevada County Airport in Grass Valley. From there it would take about an hour by car to reach Goodyears Bar.

They could only hope that Carl had not had an accident or was not the victim of foul play.

* * * *

The arsonist had left the scene, striking off down river, well south of the clearing and even further away from the apparent path of the flames. Once he was out of sight, Carl began trying to free himself from the ropes.

Carl was now in much the same situation as Dave had been in when Carmen had tied him up and left him to die in Death Valley.

The big difference was that Carl had much less time at his disposal. Instead of fearing he would die of lack of water and over-exposure to the burning hot sun over a day or two, he was in imminent peril of his life as the newly-minted fire gaining strength in the grove next to him threatened to leap across the clearing and engulf him in its devouring flames.

He thought first perhaps he could roll over and down the steep incline toward the river itself. But it was a distance away and he doubted he had time for that. Rolling up the hill and out of the direct line of fire would be even more difficult.

The fact was, Carl didn't have enough time to do much of anything. He had tried and failed to reach his phone and his bindings had been tied by an expert. Without immediate help he might as well face the fact he was doomed.

And then he heard a whirring sound—soft at first, but gradually gaining in strength. It was a firestorm—a new fire generated by the intense heat within the original flames. He had heard of these and his heart sank, believing he was a goner for sure.

But, as he watched and waited, something interesting began to happen. The intensity of the firestorm, remarkable as it seemed, created a wind effect that was actually turning the main body of the fire around in the opposite direction.

Surely the arsonist had not planned for this, Carl thought, still struggling desperately to get loose of his bindings. The man had fled in that very direction. Unless he had made it out of the woods and back up to the street by now, he would be in the path of the fire he had started.

Eventually, Carl gave up and lay still, trying to conserve his strength in case the man came back—or more hopefully—to be ready for rescue from one of his contacts.

As the wildfire continued to rage and roar away and past him, he wondered what terror and pain the arsonist might be experiencing over there—on the other side of eternity.

* * * *

Carmen, now known as Lisa, was furious. She was angry at Carl for not drinking all his spiked coffee, she was angry at the truck driver for blaring his horn at her when she passed him—but most of all she was angry at fate—for having played such a lousy trick on her.

Why! Why in God's name did everything she ever planned have to go so wrong? She was smart, she was careful—God knew she had plenty of money now. All she wanted to do was get to Canada and go to ground.

But fate would have it otherwise.

Following the unexpected incident with Carl, she continued south from Goodyears Bar toward Nevada City. She planned to stop for the night there, hopefully somewhere off the road, and get her bearings again.

She had no idea if Carl would make an attempt to follow her, but she was exhausted and would need to get some sleep before striking out for Spokane, a good two to three days to the north.

She had only gone a short way when she spotted a dirt pull off heading into a thick copse which had been spared from the recent wildfires. On a whim, she pulled off and parked behind the trees in a shady nook not visible from the road.

Sighing in relief, she pushed back her seat into a reclining position and prepared to nap.

After all, she thought. *No one can see me down here. It's quiet and peaceful. If I can sleep for a little while I might be able to get over the Or-*

egon border before I stop again.

A moment later, a deer stepped softly into the glade and stopped directly in front of her car. It was a doe, judging from the lack of antlers, and like the sea bird on Larry's boat, it seemed unafraid of her.

Their eyes locked and for a brief moment she felt at one with the wild creature. It was as if they shared both a past and a future at the same time. She envied its freedom and simplicity of choices.

Then the magical spell was broken and the animal bolted past her toward the highway. She wished more than anything she could trade places with it and run from her destiny with as much ease.

She lay back in the seat and tried to relax.

The sky overhead began to darken and she thought it might rain. There was a soft whirring and rustling sound of wind blowing in through the tall tree branches from the north. It was a soothing noise and she soon fell into a sound and seamless sleep.

Gradually the smoke thickened and then her world turned completely black.

She dreamt of the deer running free into the wilderness and wondered what her own new incarnation might be.

* * * *

An SUV was waiting for Everett and his team as soon as they landed at Nevada County Airport.

"C'mon," called Richard. "Let's go. There's no time to waste."

Their little party gathered up their gear and trudged wearily to the car.

"Who wants to drive?" Dave said. "Anybody feel up to it?"

"I'll drive," Chip said. "I actually slept pretty well on the plane. Just point me in the right direction."

Richard was already examining the GPS and plugging in the coordinates.

"Head out this way," Ev pointed toward one of the access roads. "I've been up through here before. It was a long time ago, granted. But this area hasn't changed all that much, I'll bet."

There wasn't much conversation as they drove. Each man was lost in thoughts of what had been and what might be. And what each of them might have done differently if they had only known then what they knew now.

The projected time for the drive from Nevada City to Goodyears Bar was an hour, but Chip negotiated the forty mile mountain road in a little over 45 minutes, screeching and squealing around the curves as his passengers hung on tight.

No one said a word.

As they began to draw near the area, David spoke up. "Do you all see that?"

Black smoke was curling up through the trees from the river side of the highway. The closer they got to their destination, the thicker it became, until finally they were forced to close all the windows and turn on the air conditioning to try and dispel some of the irritant.

"Oh, God," said Chip, as they neared the drop off point. "I think we must be too late."

Finally he spotted a turn out and pulled over.

"Now what," he said. "Do we go on? Or do you think we should start looking here?"

"Go a little further up," said Richard. We're not quite to Goodyears Bar yet. It looks like the smoke might actually be lessening the further north we go."

"Look," Dave said, pointing. "There's a car parked over there at the side of the road. Do we know what kind of car Carl was driving?"

"Yes," said Everett, checking his notes. "That's got to be the car that was allotted to him when he left Sacramento. I made sure I had the description."

Chip pulled over to the edge of the road and parked, and they all scrambled out.

"Is there any kind of a trail around here?" Richard said. "Do you see a way in?"

"Here," called Dave. "Here it is. This must be the path he was talking about."

Running now, the four men made their way down the dirt path toward the river. Chip sprinted ahead and as he turned a corner they could hear him shout out triumphantly.

"Here he is! He's all right! Come help me!"

They all congregated at the bottom of the hill in the midst of the little clearing that was meant to be Carl's crematorium but by happenstance became his salvation.

Carl, for his part, wanted only to get away from that terrible place. They made sure he was completely all right to be moved then they formed a little procession to assist him up and out of the depths of hell and into the safety of the SUV.

Everett Hightower was on the phone with Sacramento requesting back-up and assistance with the new fire, now blazing southward, out of control, and possibly endangering Nevada City itself.

Carl had also given them his new information about the identity of the arsonist, which confirmed Chip's speculations, and an APB was sent out for the immediate apprehension and arrest of the culprit.

Fearing now that the firestorm headed toward Nevada City might actually jump the highway, they turned toward Downieville instead, hoping to get Carl any needed medical attention and plan their next strategy.

"Do you think Jim Brown could have survived the fire?" Dave asked Carl.

"The last I saw of him he was headed south through the woods," Carl said. "The firestorm changed the direction of the flames just a few moments later. Otherwise it would have come straight for me, as he intended, and I would have been a goner.

"Dave, there's something else..." Carl hesitated, not knowing exactly how to phrase it.

"I also had an encounter with your lady friend," he said finally.

Dave looked at him quizzically. "My...?"

"The woman you were working with. What did she call herself? Carmen?"

"She's alive?" Hightower said.

"Well, at least I'm pretty sure it was her," Carl said. "I couldn't swear for certain, of course. But Richard had been telling me some things about her—and well—I think I might know who she really is."

They all looked at him, stunned by this revelation.

"What are you talking about?" Dave demanded. "What do you mean, she's still alive?"

Carl began with his overnight stay in Downieville, followed by breakfast the next morning in the little diner.

"Wait," said Dave. "You think she dosed your coffee?"

"I'm certain of it, Dave," he said. "I had only driven as far as where you found the car when I started getting sick to my stomach and woozy. Fortunately, I hadn't drunk that much of it, just a sip or so, then spat it back out in the mug. She was sitting at the next booth in the diner, watching me, when I went to the restroom. I think she believed I drank it all."

"But how did you get away from her?" Chip said. They all waited with bated breath to hear his response.

"Well, when I stopped the car, she was right behind me. She came over to the window and asked if I needed help. I recognized her as the woman from the diner. But that's not all, Dave. I think she's that woman from the cruise ship. You know the one. She looks very different, Latina, now. But something about her mannerisms just struck a vibe with me."

David Spaulding took a deep breath. He put himself back on the ship, looking down, watching an unknown woman reach out and shove his beloved Deborah into the sea in order to take her place on the lifeboat—Deb, who couldn't swim.

"Yes," he said. "I can see it now. She's a master of disguises. I think she must have changed her identity, hoping to get back into Canada somehow as a completely different person."

"Is it possible," said Richard. "Do you think it's possible she may have believed you recognized her from the ship—knew her real identity? Maybe she thought your real assignment was to apprehend her."

"You may be right about that," said Dave. "But that doesn't help us now. You say she was headed south down toward Nevada City? And this was right before the firestorm started taking the blaze in that direction?"

"Yes, that's right. But she was going like a bat out of hell," Carl said. "She nearly ran into a semi, as I remember. I don't know what happened to her after that, but she easily could have outrun the fire. She probably didn't even know it was headed in her direction."

* * * *

"So what do we do now?" Dave said. "We have not one but two perpetrators. And it looks as if they both headed south in the path of the new firestorm. Ironically, the arsonist thought he was moving away from the fire he started, but he may actually have been caught right in its path."

"But at least our arsonist is now known to the Forest Service by his real name, Jim Brown," Richard said. "Since he's been working for them they should have a complete file on him. And now they will put an immediate APB out for him. If he actually survives the fire Carl witnessed him starting, he will find himself in even greater jeopardy once he's captured. Jim—or 'Charlie' as we were calling him—was a real monster all right. But I have great confidence that the State of California will leave no stone unturned in order to seek revenge for all the harm and hurt he has caused over the years."

"I will be curious to discover if he *is* our missing 'Charlie' though," Dave said. "He might not be the only firebug out there, but this one will never be able to hide in plain sight again—as he's done all this time."

"As for the woman we've been calling Carmen," Richard added. "As Shakespeare once said 'Leave her to Heaven'—and that might be our best approach when it comes to her. She has been overtaken and killed in this latest fire—or she may be halfway back to her native Canada by now, traveling under yet another alias. We can give the authorities all we know about her, including her suspected activities on the cruise ship. But I suggest we don't pursue her any further. Not unless we come across hard information about her present whereabouts."

"So you're saying we should just do nothing?" Carl said. "After all we've been through, do we just close the book on it and go home?"

"Well," Richard said. "Would that be such a bad option? We have fulfilled our major assignment by actually finding out the identity of the arsonist, our 'needle in a haystack'. And Carmen didn't even enter into the equation. Do we really want to spend the next six months of our lives trying to figure out what fate has bestowed on these two evil beings in their next incarnation?"

"If you want my opinion," said Chip. "I tend to agree with Richard. We can give the authorities here all the information we have on both of these perps. Then, I vote we get the hell out of Dodge and count our lucky stars."

"Amen," said Carl. "The girls must be worried sick about us by now. How about it Dave? Are you ready for some good home cooking and a little rest and relaxation back in good old Pittsburgh?"

Dave smiled. "No," he said. "You guys go on back to your ladies and take a well-deserved rest." He glanced at Richard. "I think I'll hang around California a bit longer.

"After all, who knows what *karma* might have in store for me the next time around?"

ABOUT THE AUTHOR

Mary Wickizer Burgess was born in Southern California, the daughter of an attorney and justice of the peace. She spent her early life in the San Bernardino Mountains, where she rode her horse in the foothills and back byways. Later she settled with her parents on a working ranch near Redlands, California.

She married author and editor Robert Reginald (1948-2013) in 1976. With him, she established Borgo Press and spent the next thirty years in the publishing field, writing, editing and assisting in all aspects of the business.

She currently spends her time between California and Maryland with her daughter and assistant, Louise Reynnells.